HER PERFECT GAME

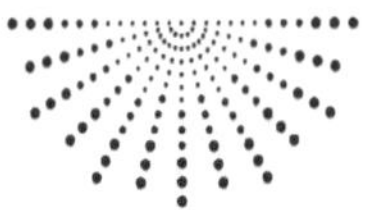

SHANNYN SCHROEDER

CONTENTS

Originally published October 2014

ISBN-13: 978-1-950640-08-9

Charlie Castle stared at the ringing phone, debating whether she should answer, but Layla had been her best friend since high school and she would think something was wrong if Charlie didn't answer. "Hey, babe, what's up?"

"Hi, Charlie," two separate voices answered.

"Felicity?"

"Yep. Layla has us all on the line. Must be something big."

Layla continued, "I had my interview for the summer internship today and you're *not* going to believe this."

"And?" Felicity asked.

Charlie heard the excitement in her friend's voice. You'd think it was Felicity's good news. "And, what?" Charlie added. "We know you got the internship. They love you."

"They offered me a job instead of the internship."

"Holy shit," Charlie said. Felicity squealed, and Charlie held the phone away from her head.

She couldn't believe it. A job with the NSA meant that Layla wouldn't be coming home after graduation, at least not to stay. The National Security Agency was based in Maryland. They'd lost Layla to the internship program for a chunk of every summer since they'd started college.

"I can't wait to tell you guys all about it. You're both going to be home for spring break, right?"

"I never left, remember?" Charlie struggled to keep the jealousy out of her voice. She was truly happy for her friends. If she had taken school more seriously, she probably could've kept her scholarship like Layla had. Felicity's parents could afford to send her anywhere.

Felicity interrupted her thoughts. "Well, that was the plan, but don't you think in light of your excellent news we should celebrate? We should all meet up for a proper spring break. Let's go somewhere touristy and get drunk and have fun."

Charlie couldn't believe her ears. "Okay, who are you? Hey, Layla, are you sure you dialed right?"

"Yes, she dialed right, smart-ass. Every year we talk about going somewhere to have fun. This is our last spring break. After this, we're all out in the real world. We might be scattered all over the country for our jobs. I heard a girl talking about going to South Padre Island in Texas. Let's go."

Charlie listened to her friends making plans. Layla was going to start driving now. Charlie couldn't go. Not only could she not afford something like that, but if she went, they would take one look at her and know something was wrong.

"What about you, Charlie?"

"I have a con planned for next weekend." She'd used every extra penny she had to pay for the registration.

"So come for part of the week," Layla offered.

Charlie tried to figure out what to say. She'd planned on telling her friends in her own time, like after they had graduated.

"Charlotte, we hear you breathing. What's going on?" Layla was persistent.

"I think Ethan has something special planned for this week." She knew her friends had never cared for Ethan. What was one more lie? If she'd told them Ethan had dumped her, they would demand she come to spring break. If she went on the trip, they would find out that she'd dropped out of school.

Plus, she needed to go to the convention. The hackfest called to her. The prize money would set her straight for months. It would also be her ticket to Def Con in the summer. Adding the hackfest win to her résumé might even help her get a real job. Anything to get her life moving again.

"It won't be the same without you." Layla sounded concerned.

"I know, but you guys go ahead and have a great time. I expect you to have my share of the fun too. Especially Felicity. Get that girl laid."

"Hey, *that girl* is listening. What makes you think I need to get laid?"

Charlie snickered. Subject changed. "When

was the last time you had an orgasm with someone other than yourself?"

"Some of us have discriminating taste."

"Yeah, and some of us are too shy to speak to anyone with a dick."

"Now, girls..." Layla, always the peacemaker.

Felicity continued to talk about booking a room, but Charlie tuned it out. Her brain had already moved on to the finishing touches needed on her costume for the convention, and her fingers itched to log on to the convention site to find the day's scavenger hunt clue. When her friends said good-bye, she mumbled a response and hung up.

Clue first, then costume. Although the cosplay part of the convention was fun and fed her playful side, she needed to ensure she'd be part of the hacking competition. It was invitation only, and in order to score the invite, she needed to complete the scavenger hunt. A new clue was posted daily, supposedly at random times. She, however, created an algorithm to figure out when the clue would post. Any halfway decent computer geek could do the same, so she was sure she didn't have that much of a leg up. She was just beating the guys who weren't serious about it anyway.

She pulled out her laptop, the secondary one only used for hacking. The computer itself held nothing personal to trace it back to her. Hacking wasn't something she did to cause trouble, and in truth, except for her first foray into hacking when she was a freshman, everything she did now was just to keep her skills up. She hadn't considered it a career move until she stumbled on the scavenger hunt. The hackfest was being sponsored by a group of companies from software creators to security experts. If she could prove herself there, maybe a degree wouldn't be so important.

She logged on to the convention website and clicked through to the events page to find the clue. Nothing. She scanned the page twice and then rubbed her eyes. Her algorithm hadn't been wrong yet. She hit the refresh button and then she saw it: a small numerical thirteen on the lower right corner of the page. It hadn't been there the first two times she looked.

Thirteen? What kind of clue was that? She pulled out her notebook that contained the puzzles she'd already solved. The convention started in five days. The organizers must've decided to up the difficulty. Scanning through the other pages of the site, she found each had a number. Now all she had to do was figure out what they meant.

 walked through her apartment keenly aware of the quiet. Her roommate Amy usually left the TV or the radio playing. Sometimes both. She glanced to the kitchen counter and saw two wineglasses sitting near the sink.

Oh goody, Amy had her boyfriend over. Again. She was trying not to be a bitch about it, but the man was in their place more than Charlie was, and he wasn't paying for anything. What made it worse was that he'd eat her food. Like her favorite yogurt and then not even have the decency to offer a fake apology.

She yanked her hair free from her ponytail and kicked her shoes off, nudging them close to the door so she could easily find them in the morning. Work had beaten her down tonight. As much as she hated the morning shift at a coffee shop, she could at least understand why people might be rude to her. She tended to land on the far side of testy without her morning dose of caffeine. But at seven in the evening?

Tonight had been one of those nights where she could do nothing right. Even if she thought it had been right, the customers didn't agree. All she wanted was a hot shower and some time to play *The Order of Resskaar*. As she grabbed her pajamas from her room, she heard quiet moans coming from the other side of the wall she shared with Amy.

Good thing she owned an excellent pair of noise canceling headphones. Her dry spell would make hearing them go at it difficult at best. She didn't like being jealous, but it had been way too long since she'd experienced a screaming orgasm, regardless of what her good friends believed.

Part of that was because Ethan had never hit the mark that some men did. He hadn't been a bad lover, exactly, just not as good as others. She sighed and started the hot water. She needed to flush men from her mind. Only two months remained in the school year and then she wouldn't be able to hold her secret anymore.

Telling everyone—her mom, Layla, Felicity—that she had dropped out of school would sting a whole lot less if she at least had a plan figured out. Having time to implement that plan would be even better.

After her shower, Charlie went back to her room and tuned out the sounds of the squeaky bed banging against the wall. She booted up her computer and put on her headphones. She hoped Win was online because she could really use a friend tonight. He'd take her mind off her lame job and whiny customers. And if it was a quiet night, maybe they could sneak away for some private time.

So much for flushing men from her mind.

But Win didn't count. He was a virtual man. Well, she was pretty sure he was a man in the real world too, but she only knew him virtually, as a dwarven mage. And it would stay that way unless she could finally convince him to join her at the convention. They would have so much fun together. Even outside the bedroom.

As the home screen welcomed her, Charlie began to relax. She turned the volume up on her stereo to drown out Amy's noise. She preferred to listen to music while she played and just read the conversation on screen. In her head, the characters had natural voices, and the computerized version never sounded real enough, so she ignored them.

She shot a message to Win. *You around?*

No one answered, so she wandered through the virtual forest looking for the rest of the members of her guild. At least two others were logged on. As she walked, she noticed that her friends had picked up some treasures while she'd been at work. Looking at the loot, she saw things that they had all agreed were unnecessary for their mission. She sighed. This happened every now and then, especially when new members joined the guild.

She didn't try to restrict membership, but she had guidelines for what she expected the group to be. They were called The Guardians after all. Stealing from people and taking things the guild didn't need went against everything they stood for. She searched for the tree that would have the items tied to the boughs out of sight. When she found the bag, she took it with her to the village. Starting at the orphanage, she handed out items that others would use to barter to stay alive.

That's when she ran into Kraven. He was the newest member of the guild, and she suspected he was the one responsible for the bag.

What are you doing? That's my stuff.

I'm spreading the wealth. That's what we do.

Do you know how many people I had to go up against to earn that?

I have no idea. What were you planning to do with it?

Save it to exchange for things we'll need. There are only a few more missions until we reach the final one. We'll need supplies to help Resskaar.

I'm in no hurry to reach the final battle. I told you that when you asked to join my guild.

Your guild? I assumed it was Win's guild. He was the one who invited me.

Win invited you after talking to me.

Figures. I'm out.

He snatched the bag from her hand and took off with whatever of his loot remained. He sneered at a few of the villagers, but he knew better than to take what she had just given them.

Confronting Kraven left a bad taste in her mouth. She'd come to the game tonight to find refuge, not a fight. Now, however, a fight might make her feel better. She checked the mission status. The others from her guild had logged off, except Kraven. She was on her own. She marched to the edge of town and took off in a run to find the band of marauders she knew had taken up camp.

The thieves stormed every village they came across until they left nothing but a shell behind. She knew she wouldn't be able to take them all on, but her health was near one hundred percent, so she could handle a couple before retreating.

In the distance, she saw the small campfire. As she neared the edge of the camp, she crept along the tree line. If she could find the right vantage point, she could take out half the group without breaking a sweat. Spotting a low-hanging branch, she jumped and climbed. When she found a good bough, one with enough coverage to hide her, but still allow a clean shot with her arrow, she settled in. As she surveyed the group below her, a ping told her one of her guild had just logged on.

Win.

It was silly that her heartbeat quickened at the sight of his name, but every time she saw it, it was like she knew she'd be able to see a good friend.

Hey, gorgeous, where are you? Not in our cave.

She typed back quickly. *In a tree about to cause some trouble. Want to join me?*

On my way.

That was one of the many reasons she loved Win. He didn't ask questions; he just came. She got comfortable on her branch while she waited for him and developed a plan. She knew which men she'd need to take out first, and now that Win would have her back, she could attack, and he could swoop in and take their cache.

By the end of the night, she'd at least make a few other people secure, and that might be enough to make up for her evening.

Moments later, she saw the rustle of a bush and knew Win had arrived. He always knew where to find her. She launched her first arrow, nailing one soldier's shoulder. She took out two more before the others realized what was happening. Unfortunately, they figured out quickly where she was and came at her.

She jumped from her branch and led them away from Win's position. Without the rest of their guild, he didn't stand a chance against these monsters. She might be able to outrun them. It seemed like a good plan until one shot a rock and hit her in the head. A breath later they were on her, kicking her and throwing more stones. Her life energy was waning fast. She tried to scramble to her feet, but it was no use. They outnumbered her and had her surrounded.

Suddenly a flash fire burst around her and she sighed. If it had been the enemy, she'd be in flames. This was Win's doing. The group tossed a few more rocks in her direction, but gave up when they realized that it wasn't worth the health points to get past the fire.

Thanks for having my back.

That was a stupid move. You okay?

Been better.

Then the flames died and Win stood there staring at her, a stuffed bag flung over his shoulder. The mission was a success.

Come on. He leaned over to pick her up.

In the quiet of her bedroom, Charlie laughed out loud. Win was a dwarf, a short, round guy about half her height. He was strong, though, and he hefted her and ran back to their cave.

You need to be more careful, Laura.

Win almost never called her by name. It suddenly struck her as weird. She called him Win all the time, but he never called her Laura.

They didn't speak again until they were safe and Win healed her. He was always doing that, taking care of her. Not that she didn't do her share of saving his ass, but he was a healer and she was a warrior. They made a hell of a team.

When she'd regained her strength, she sat in front of the fire Win had built for them.

Have you thought about coming to the con next week?

I told you, I don't know if I can.

If it's money, you can crash in my room. All you need is registration.

We'll see.

She winked at him. *It'll be fun.* Then she curled up to sleep. Win lay beside her and everything in her calmed.

If only she had that in real life.

CHAPTER TWO

For the rest of the weekend, Jonah Best was taunted by the words that seemed to have typed themselves on the screen to Charlie. *We'll see.* What the hell was he thinking? He couldn't go to the con to meet Charlie. She'd be pissed to find out who he was, and he'd lose this —her—again. In the game, they were perfect together. They fought side by side. When they disagreed, they fought each other, but the anger never lasted. They'd learned to listen to each other.

So different than three years ago. Back then, neither of them had listened.

He hadn't gone back to the game since saying those words to her because he didn't want to hear to her harassment. And he couldn't commit to going to the con either. Then, early Monday morning, the decision was made for him.

His boss, Kyle Zimmerman, called him into his office.

"What's up?"

Zimmerman sat on the arm of the couch. The office wasn't like most. Instead of a monstrous desk and stiff chairs, Kyle's office was comfortable. Jonah flopped into one of the armchairs and settled in for what he thought would be a conversation about the next generation of games.

"Pack your bags. You're going back to your old stomping grounds."

"What?"

"Chicago. Jaime's sick and can't go to the hackfest. And since the whole thing was your idea, it only makes sense for you to fill in."

"Are you sure that's a good idea? I might know some of the competitors. Like you said, it's my old stomping grounds." Jonah shifted in the chair, suddenly not as comfortable as he thought.

"You brought the idea of sponsorship to me. We both know that the winner of the competition isn't going to be the only talent there. Other sponsors will have representation on site. We can't afford to lose out."

Jonah knew Kyle was right. This kind of competition brought out the best hackers. They could assess things that wouldn't show on a résumé or in transcripts. They needed people who could think on the fly to work in their newly expanded R & D department, and they always needed security people.

"Your flight is booked for Wednesday morning."

Jonah had no idea what his expression said to Kyle, but it must not have looked good.

"Think of it as a free vacation. Spend some

time with hackers. Check out the skimpy outfits on cosplayers. Have a few drinks. Have fun, but do what you have to do to recruit."

While he knew many people would dress in costume to look like their favorite movie and gaming characters, it didn't do much for Jonah. "I'm not a recruiter, Kyle. I can pick out the best, but I don't know that I'll be able to convince anyone to join us."

"Lay the groundwork. That's all we need you to do. We'll handle the rest."

Jonah left Kyle's office and went back to his own work space. It wasn't an office or a cubicle. When Kyle designed the office, he wanted everyone to be able to interact, so the old loft space was left open. Drafting tables were shoved together for conference space, usually a team talking story line over cheap Chinese food or pizza. Each team member had a computer station that they worked from, but they shared everything. It wasn't unusual to find one of his teammates at his station.

So he shouldn't have been surprised to see Tim sitting in his chair waiting for news of his meeting with Kyle. As much as Jonah enjoyed the laid-back atmosphere of his job, sometimes it was inconvenient.

"So?"

Jonah shrugged. "I'm going to Chicago for the rest of the week, so you need to keep the team on track while I'm gone. We're still having problems with *Resskaar*. People are getting in and fucking with abilities. You need to find the issue and create a patch before there are bigger problems."

Tim swiveled in the chair. "Bigger problems like what?"

"I don't want to know. That's my point. Right now, the few I've seen are guys figuring out how to steal the same thing more than once or restore their health without a healer."

Tim stood and shrugged. "What's the big deal about that?"

"It's not a big deal yet. But players will start to notice, and if one guy makes changes, others will follow. It could fuck with the whole system." Jonah took the seat Tim vacated.

"I know that, but that game's been out for a couple of years. Why waste the time and energy when we should be focusing on the new version?"

"Because we have loyal players on this version. We want them to follow us to the next. If they think the world is unstable because of a few hackers, we lose customers." He spun in his chair and hoped Tim would take the hint.

"Whatever, man. We'll get in and figure it out."

The hacking bothered Jonah more than it probably should. Every game had people who hacked to make modifications. But *Resskaar* was the first game Jonah had worked on and he had a soft spot for it. It wasn't a perfect game. It had plenty of issues and glitches that they'd had to fix over the years, but he loved the world and the premise of the story.

And this was the game that had led him back to Charlie.

~

WEDNESDAY CAME TOO SOON FOR JONAH. HE FELT like he was leaving too many things unfinished at work. He was only going to be gone for five days, but the hacking issues in *Resskaar* had doubled since the weekend. He'd checked forums to try to find who was spreading the information, but he'd had no luck. Now he had to trust his team to handle it.

As the plane touched down in Chicago, Jonah turned on his phone and checked for messages from Tim. Nothing. His fingers itched to be on a keyboard, searching for the problem. He'd spent most of the last two nights doing just that and he was exhausted. The idea of being smashed in throngs of people at a convention made him cringe. Even at his best, he didn't like crowds.

He followed the passengers off the plane as they moved like cattle; the bodies pressing against him tightened every muscle. The airport wasn't much better. After walking probably a mile and a half to get his suitcase and find a cab, he was finally on his way to the hotel. While the cabbie dodged traffic on the Kennedy, Jonah checked his e-mail as the downtown skyline came into view.

They passed the WinTrust building, and he tried to remember what mural had been there the last time he'd seen it. It was one of those things he had overlooked at his time downtown while in college. He'd been aware of its presence, but had never paid attention to the art. This time, he found himself setting his phone down to look.

The John Hancock and the Willis Tower stood tall, their tops not visible because of cloud cover. Maybe this weekend, he'd take a trip to the sky deck at Willis Tower. The glass platform had opened his last year here and he'd been too cool for touristy things. As they pulled into downtown, the cab became darker with the tall buildings concealing the meager sunlight. He'd arrived late enough in the day that they'd missed rush hour, but the traffic moved slowly through downtown.

Even with the sluggish traffic, Jonah realized he'd missed this city. He hadn't returned in the nearly three years since graduating. He'd almost forgotten what had drawn him here in the first place. The cab pulled up to the hotel. Jonah paid the fare and grabbed his luggage. After checking in, he dropped his bags in his room and doubled back downstairs to assess the conference room that would host the first challenge for the hack-fest. The first two nights they booked large rooms because they expected a huge turnout, but only the best would move on to subsequent chal-lenges, so the last night would be held in a smaller room. His biggest concern was making sure the power was adequate.

While waiting in the lobby to speak to one of the conference organizers, Jonah saw her. Even after three years, Charlie was unmistakable. Her messy blond hair was only partially hidden by the knit cap she wore. With her black backpack slung over one shoulder, she checked in.

He knew she saw him, felt it in the air, but she took her room key and walked to the conference registration table. He waited, but even after getting her registration material, she didn't turn to acknowledge him. And why should she? He'd left without a word.

He strode up behind her and called, "Charlie."

There was a brief hitch in her stride before she turned, but when she faced him, her bright smile dazzled him. "Best! What the hell are you doing here?"

She threw her arms around him in a too-friendly hug.

Best. He'd forgotten that she'd always called him by his last name. Except in bed. Then he was Jonah. He forced images of Charlie in his bed away and answered, "My company is sponsoring the hackfest."

"Hackfest?"

She never did play dumb well. "Drop the act. Yes, it's supposed to be secret, but I have access to the registrants. I knew you'd be here."

"Sponsorship, huh? So that means you're not competing?" Hopefulness filled her face.

"I haven't decided." No, he hadn't planned to compete, but he liked to push her buttons.

Her eyes narrowed slightly. "Wouldn't that be a conflict of interest?"

"We sponsored the prize money. A third party

created the challenges and will determine final winners. I'm here to observe."

Relief came into her eyes. "I guess I'll see you later then."

"How about a drink?"

Her lips curved but didn't quite make a full smile. "We'll see. I have a busy week planned."

He watched her walk away. He'd expected her to be pissed off, maybe a little hurt, but she showed no signs of either emotion. It had been almost three years. He supposed it was possible that his leaving didn't have nearly the same impact on her as it had him. For some reason, that bothered him more. He had five days to set things right with Charlie. He didn't know exactly what that would mean, but he knew that it was something that he'd been working toward for more than a year.

As he stood thinking about Charlie, one of the conference organizers caught his arm and offered to show him the room for tonight.

WHEN THE ELEVATOR DOORS CLOSED, CHARLIE released a shuddering breath. Of all the things she'd hoped to experience this week, a reunion with Jonah Best didn't even come close to making the list. As soon as she'd entered the lobby, she noticed him. How could she not? For a few brief months three years ago, Jonah had been her friend, her lover, her mentor, her lifeline. No one had ever had such an impact on her.

Part of her was a little pissed that he still looked so good. After he'd left, she'd wanted to believe that he'd get old and ugly, as if three years would make that much of a difference. The other part of her couldn't control being attracted to him. He still affected her without even trying. She attempted to steady her breathing and lower her heart rate. What the hell was she going to do?

The hackfest was her best shot of doing something she loved with her life, but she couldn't go up against Jonah. First of all, he'd taught her most of what she knew about hacking. Second, he was a huge distraction. There was too much between them. Too much history, too much emotion, too much...God, she didn't even have the words to describe the tornado swirling in her chest.

By the time she got to her room, her hands were steady enough that she got the key card to work on the first try. She wanted to talk to someone about running into Jonah, but who? She'd never told anyone about her relationship with him. It had all happened so fast, and she was in such a bad place that she'd wanted to have him all to herself. Layla and Felicity might recognize the name, but they'd assume he was just some guy she'd fucked. He'd never been that.

There was only one person she could think of that she could vent to. After dumping her bag on the bed, she booted up her computer and logged on. Of course, it was still afternoon, so Win wouldn't be playing the game, but she could leave him a message. He'd left her one, early this morning.

Hey, gorgeous, you might want to stay offline for a bit. Ran into Kraven. He's really pissed about you taking his stuff.

Kraven was the least of her worries right now.

Thanks for the heads-up. What would I have to do to convince you to come to Chicago? I might sound desperate, but I just saw my ex. Complicated stuff. If you're here, I'll be less likely to do something stupid.

She clicked send, not too worried about how desperate she might sound. Win was a good friend, and this week, especially, she'd need a good friend.

Charlie logged off and sorted through her registration materials. She'd been so focused on the hackfest that she hadn't really looked at the panels she might want to attend. She scrolled through the schedule, but the bold date at the top of the page glared at her.

Three years ago today.

Why couldn't this con be any other week? Spring break landed all over for different schools. Why this week? It would take every ounce of effort to concentrate and forget about Sylvie.

But the damn date at the top of the page wouldn't let her go. She glanced at the clock. Three years ago, what had Sylvie been doing? Who had she been thinking of? Why didn't she call someone, anyone, but especially Charlie?

Instead, Sylvie jumped from the water tower in her small hometown and died alone.

Three years ago today.

CHAPTER THREE

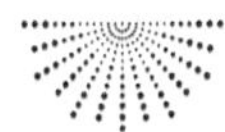

At eight fifty, Jonah couldn't help but stare at the clock. The first challenge was set to start in less than ten minutes, but he hadn't seen Charlie since their run-in in the lobby. He worried that his presence might've scared her off. That hadn't been his intention. He'd just wanted to hear her voice. Plus, he didn't want the shock of seeing him to throw her off her game tonight.

Eight fifty-five. Most of the seats were filled. About fifty people sat in the stuffy room and he could count on one hand how many were female. Just as the moderator grabbed the door to shut it, Charlie squeezed past, flashing her invitation, and took the seat nearest the door.

She wore an oversized army jacket and a baseball cap low on her face. He had a sick feeling about her reasons for the semi-disguise. She quickly set up her laptop and pulled an energy drink from her bag. Most players had similar drinks at their stations. It was a staple of the community.

The directions were read for the first challenge. Jonah tuned them out. He didn't need to know what the goal was as much as he needed to watch how the players approached the task. They had one hour to meet the goal. The top thirty would move on to round two.

As soon as start was called, everyone began typing furiously at their keyboards. Except for a select few, Charlie being one of them. She was scrolling through code. While most players would barge through the front door to leave their mark, she was taking her time, searching for a loose basement window. *That's my girl.*

The fleeting thought hit him hard. Charlie had listened to almost everything he'd said about hacking. She was smart, sometimes unfocused, but she had great intuition. He stopped by her table, snatched the energy drink, and replaced it with a bottle of water. She shot a glare at him but didn't speak.

No one else seemed to notice, so he moved on because he didn't want anyone to accuse him of favoritism. Even though he definitely had a soft spot for Charlie.

Twenty minutes in, the first five players were done and packing up. They knew they were a lock, so they didn't wait for judgment. Jonah waited at the door for them to exit and give them their pass to the next round. He waited anxiously as the stack of passes dwindled. He knew Charlie could do this. It was a simple hack. What was she doing?

As he had the thought, she shut her laptop

with a quiet click and headed for the door. Handing him the bottle of water, she said, "Don't touch my stuff. I don't need you to take care of me."

Her eyes told a slightly different story. She'd been crying. "We both know that when you drink that shit, you get all hopped up and then you might do something stupid."

"Like you?" Her quip came as quickly as her smirk.

He probably had that coming, but he'd really been thinking about her bad habits from the past. She'd suck down energy drinks, and then when she couldn't sleep, she'd light a joint. She had no balance for anything in her life. But she seemed to be doing better. "How about that drink?"

"Sorry, I have a date." And she slid through the door without a backward glance.

He continued to hand out the remaining passes and thought about what would make Charlie cry. Being at a con should make her happy. This was the kind of place where she would thrive. She liked crowds and conversation and the craziness of fans.

He checked his watch, and as his gaze slid over the date, he made the connection. Charlie had been crying over Sylvie. Now he really felt like shit for talking about her doing something stupid. Charlie wasn't immune to doing stupid things, but he shouldn't have joked with her if she was hurting.

The first challenge wrapped up with some people grumbling about the scores and the challenge itself. The moderator basically told them better luck next year.

Jonah headed out and thought about going to the convention main floor. Certainly there would be plenty to see and do, but he really didn't want to run into Charlie with her sad eyes and whatever guy she had on her arm, so he went back to his room.

In the elevator, his phone pinged letting him know that Charlie had logged on to *Resskaar*. Shit. Hadn't he told her to stay offline for a few days? Kraven had been furious when they'd run into each other. He'd been screaming, and nothing Jonah had said would calm him. They'd actually gotten into a fight.

The worry about Kraven faded and a new thought came to Jonah. Charlie had said she had a date. Why the hell was she online?

In his room, he logged in to the game and checked messages first. *Laura: I might sound desperate, but I just saw my ex. Complicated stuff. If you're here, I'll be less likely to do something stupid.* He laughed. So she was afraid of doing something stupid with him and she thought inviting Win would prevent that. No way could he come clean about his online identity now. Kraven still appeared as part of their guild, and Jonah saw he was also logged on.

Not good for Charlie. Jonah took off through the woods and into the village to find her. She had a habit of taking off and starting new missions without being in full health and hoping she'd get what she'd need on the way. He went to the house where she was supposed to be and called out to her, but didn't get an answer.

In the back room, he saw why. Kraven was pummeling her. As Win came through the door, Kraven held Charlie's avatar Laura by the throat. With one swipe of his hand, he tore away her clothes.

What the fuck? Nothing in the program would allow that.

Now you'll learn why bitches don't belong in game. A cunt's only good for one thing.

Jonah rushed forward and slammed Win's little body into Kraven. Laura slumped to the floor, and Jonah used every keystroke and bit of health energy he had to send Kraven up in flames. As soon as Kraven was a pile of ash, Jonah watched his own avatar flop down.

Jonah logged off and grabbed his phone while he entered the back end of the game. Something was wrong with the code. When Tim answered, he was already searching.

"What's up, Jonah? No luck picking up chicks?"

"Shut up and listen. I need you to get into the system right now. Player named Kraven just tried to rape a woman in game. Find out who the fuck he is. Now!"

Tim began to mumble as if just coming to attention, but Jonah heard him clacking away on the keyboard. While Tim looked for Kraven's identity, Jonah searched for how the asshole modified the game.

Sexual activity was allowed in the game, and

players had choices to hook up, but nowhere would he have allowed a rape to happen. There wasn't even nudity. They permitted some foreplay on screen and then it was pretty much fade to black. Jonah had no idea how much this guy fucked with the system in order to rip away Charlie's—Laura's—clothes. Jonah shook his head. It wasn't Charlie, not really. It had been her character Laura.

He scrambled through lines of code, and allowing images of Laura stripped bare into his head caused another thought. He'd just abandoned Charlie.

Again.

His fingers froze and guilt smacked him. No, he couldn't think about Charlie now. She was a tough girl. Finding how Kraven had been able to do this was a priority.

CHARLIE STARED AT THE SCREEN. WHAT THE FUCK just happened? She looked at her character lying on the dirty floor of the house. Her hand hovered over the keyboard, shaking. She didn't know what to do.

Win?

She didn't even know why she called to him. She'd watched him disappear almost as quickly as Kraven had. The burst of magic from Win had been surreal. She'd never witnessed anything like it, and she'd hung out with a lot of mages over the course of the last two years. None of them wielded that kind of power.

Rather than use her last bit of energy to return to her cave, she just logged off, leaving Laura's prone body on the floor. She'd deal with it tomorrow. All she'd wanted when she came back to her room was a little escape. Nearly getting raped was not on the agenda. The whole experience was bizarre. Nothing felt right in the game tonight.

She closed her laptop and changed her clothes. Her eyes landed on her Laura Nim costume and her stomach churned. It wasn't a fancy outfit like a lot of the cosplayers would have. It was a simple costume that matched her in-game persona. One that she'd just had ripped from her body.

A shudder ran through her. First, Jonah popped up, then memories of Sylvie, now this. There was no way her night could get worse. She grabbed her room key and some cash and headed down to the bar.

The hotel bar held an odd mix of people. Most were there from the con, but businessmen in their suits, ties barely loosened at the neck also dotted the room. She saw their wary looks at the con-goers. Some were outright amused; others appeared concerned. She grabbed a beer and sat at a table by herself.

Being alone here was much better than being in her room. Here, at least, she was among her people, even if she chose not to interact. Jedis, superheroes, and Trekkies surrounded her. The movie people talked to comic book people and gamers. No rivalries, just pure enjoyment.

The first beer went down smoothly, and she waved a waitress over to order another. She couldn't really afford to drink here. Beer that would normally cost a little more than a buck a bottle from the store was priced more than four times that. It definitely wasn't in her budget. She scanned the room. Maybe she could start up a conversation with a guy who would buy the next round for her.

Charlie felt him before she saw Jonah. That weird feeling of being watched without it being creepy. He took the seat across from her without invitation. As the waitress walked by, he pointed to Charlie's bottle and held up two fingers. She wanted to be irritated by his presence, but she couldn't. She needed a friendly face. Jonah's was definitely friendly.

She smiled. *Look at that. I'm getting a beer, and I didn't have to do any phony flirting.*

"Thought you had a date."

She lifted a shoulder. "Didn't work out."

He scanned her face, starting at her eyes, glancing down to her lips, and back up. His gaze held there, searching.

"What?" She barely kept the nervousness from her voice. When he looked at her like that, she felt like he was reaching all the way to her soul.

"How are you?"

"Fine."

He reached out and laid a hand on her arm.

"No, how are you really doing? I know this week is hard for you."

Whoa. She hadn't expected that. She raised her bottle. "Today is the third anniversary of Sylvie's death." She slugged back the last bit of beer. "I'm doing better than she is."

Sylvie had been her roommate freshman year. After she broke up with her boyfriend, he posted revenge porn. Sylvie couldn't handle the repercussions, especially since she came from a small town and a religious family, so she committed suicide. When Charlie wanted to clear her name and erase the pics, it had been Jonah who taught her about hacking.

Jonah shook his head. "How's school?"

Charlie plucked at the label on the bottle. The alcohol was hitting her and she enjoyed the slight buzz. She debated whether she should be honest, and really what did it matter? Jonah already knew all the rest of her secrets. But then he'd look at her like a loser. Someone who didn't finish what she'd started. He'd know he'd been right to leave her, and she couldn't stomach that disappointment now, so she lied. "Fine."

She moved back in her chair. Jonah sitting close was doing uncomfortable things to her. The waitress came and set the bottles on the table. Jonah signed the purchase to his room. 614. Two floors above hers.

"That's good. Any ideas about what you plan to do after graduation?"

"Not really." That's why she needed the hackfest. Showing her skills to the right people might lead somewhere.

"You should send your résumé to my company. We're looking to expand." He drank from his bottle and then asked, "So what have you been doing? Besides playing barista."

She squinted at him because she was pretty sure she hadn't mentioned her job.

"Relax. I'm not stalking you. You're wearing your apron in your Facebook photo."

She hated that picture. "So you're not really stalking, just online stalking? Yet you're here, at my table in the bar."

"I came to the bar to get a drink. You told me you had a date. And as far as online stalking goes, are you really going to tell me that you don't check on your exes from time to time?"

Charlie knew it was more than a vague question. He was trying to open the door on their relationship. She saw it for what it was. In truth, she didn't seek out information about other exes. Just him. He would always be the one who got away. "Sometimes."

She took the beer he bought her and drank. This whole situation should be awkward, but it wasn't. She was having a beer with her ex-boyfriend and neither one of them acted like it was weird. Jonah always put her at ease. "So what's it like being out in the real world?"

"I'm working at Enigma, but I guess you know that since I told you my company was sponsoring the hackfest. I got the job right after graduation and I really like it. It's a small company, but we're growing." He halted there, like he had to rethink what he was about to say. "I'm on a team that checks security for some of our games. Most of the games are RPGs. You'd probably like them. Role-playing was always your thing."

"Yeah, what do work on?"

"Right now, *The Order of Resskaar*." He took a drink and waited.

She wanted to play it cool. He'd said he wasn't stalking her, and there were like thousands of people who were logged on at any given time. "I play *Resskaar*. It's my go-to for relaxation."

"Have you completed it yet?"

"Nope. I'm not in any hurry."

They finished their drinks, and Jonah ordered another round. They spent the next hour talking and laughing. She was able to forget her in-game assault and her past. The night became filled with the enjoyment of hanging out with a friend. When the bottles were empty, Charlie reached for her pocket.

"I think you've had enough. Let me walk you to your room."

Oh, man. Those were the words she'd wanted to hear, even though she knew it wasn't wise, and his brain wasn't working in the same direction. "Okay."

She was a little unsteady on her feet, so Jonah held on to her. He was quiet on the elevator ride, but she inched closer to him. The peace of being with him after her miserable gaming experience made her feel warm and fuzzy. Or maybe that was the alcohol. She looked at Jonah's arm on her and spoke with honesty. "I missed you."

"I've missed you too."

The elevator dinged on the fourth floor, and Jonah ushered her out and down the hall. Their steps shushed against the carpet, and Charlie wanted to talk, say something, but she didn't know what. At her room, she slid the key card in, and as she pushed the door open, she tugged Jonah inside.

"What are you doing, Charlie?"

She wrapped her arms around his neck and breathed in his scent. "I don't want to be alone."

Charlie held her breath, waiting for him to push her away, but he didn't. His arms came around her and stroked her back. Memories flooded her brain. Jonah holding her, touching her, kissing her senseless. She'd give almost anything to have that again, even if it was only for a night. To feel grounded again.

She turned her head slightly and brushed her lips against his warm neck, and his hands paused on her back. She pressed on, though, kissing his jaw and loving the rough feel of the stubble.

"Charlie."

"Just kiss me, Jonah."

She didn't look into his eyes, afraid to know what she'd find, but she knew he wanted to kiss her. If for no other reason, out of sheer curiosity. She kept her eyes closed as she tilted her head.

His lips met hers with tenderness at first. Then they became more insistent, and she softened against him, inviting his tongue into her mouth. His hand reached up and cradled the back of her head, and she wanted more. This heady feeling wouldn't last the night, but Jonah could give her more.

She tugged at his T-shirt, searching for his warm skin. When her fingers met his flesh, he jerked back. "Charlie."

But she didn't stop.

He grabbed her hands. "Charlie." Then he waited for her to meet his eyes. "We're not doing this."

She swallowed hard. His steel gray eyes sparked with lust. She didn't misread the signs. He wanted her. "Why not? Got a girlfriend?"

"No girlfriend. You're well passed halfway to drunk. I don't want you to do something you're going to regret in the morning." He grabbed her shoulders and turned her toward the bed. "Get some sleep and we'll talk tomorrow."

"What if I don't want to talk tomorrow?"

He sighed. "Then I guess we won't."

She crawled on top of the covers. "Will you stay and talk for a while if I promise not to molest you?"

He glanced to the other side of the room. "Sure." He scooted the armchair a little closer to the bed.

"There's room here." She patted the bed beside her.

He simply shook his head.

"Who is it that you don't trust—me or you? I already gave my word."

He laughed and stretched his legs out in front

of him. The light from the hall cast him in shadows. Between his dark hair and black T-shirt and jeans, he blended into the dark.

She tucked her hands under her head as she lay on her side to watch him talk. "Tell me about the people you work with."

Jonah accommodated her again and spoke in quiet tones until she became sleepy and struggled to keep her eyes open. He stood, leaned over, and kissed her head.

"Hey, Best?"

"Yeah?"

"I'd never regret you."

Another heavy sigh came from him, but she didn't know how to interpret it. Then she heard the door close with a quiet thunk.

CHAPTER FOUR

The following morning, Charlie woke with a slight headache and case of cotton mouth. Her gloom from the night before had lifted, and after brushing her teeth, she felt human again. She'd had a good time with Jonah. The anxiety she'd expected to feel around him never surfaced. It was like the last three years were erased, and they were just Best and Castle again. Without the sex.

That part bothered her. She hadn't been drunk. Maybe a little more than buzzed, but she was in control of her faculties and she remembered telling him to come in, pulling him into her room. And he hadn't shied away from kissing her. But then he'd kept his distance. It was probably for the best. He'd left her so she shouldn't want him. Damn hormones.

But he made everything easy. After the way he'd left, it shouldn't be so easy.

She made herself a barely decent cup of coffee in her room and stared at her costume. Last night, she'd had a fellow player, a teammate, rip it from her body. She questioned whether she wanted to don the real thing. No one on the con floor would tear her clothes off, but it would be a reminder, wouldn't it? She shook her head. She was overthinking again.

Tying her hair back in pigtails, she began her transformation into Laura Nim. Long hair would get in the way of shooting her arrows accurately. Then she took her time spreading the teal body paint on. Unlike many others, her outfit wasn't skimpy. Because of this, she only had to paint her arms, the top of her chest, her neck, and face.

Once the paint was set, she shimmied into the faux leather pants and eased on her vest. She added her pointy ears that would signify her elven nature. With her costume in place, she studied herself in the mirror. The only thing that would really finish it would be the amulet that Win had given her in game. It was the only treasure that she'd kept for herself. Mostly because it had been a gift from Win.

But she wasn't creative enough to make jewelry in the real world. She wasn't even a costume person. Her clothes came right off the rack, so she wouldn't be winning any contests today, but that wasn't really the point, at least not for her. She dressed up so that for a little while, she could escape reality. Before having to cover up and enter a den of dudes for the hackfest later tonight, she could be a sexy archer elf. She'd run into a few *Resskaar* players, and they'd have some drinks and talk about their love for the game.

That's what this week was really about. Being with like-minded people. The hackfest competition and the hope of networking to find a job were bonuses.

She grabbed her bow and quiver of arrows to complete her ensemble. Then she headed downstairs for a day of panels and discussions and fun. She was determined to have some fun this week. Regardless of how Sylvie had ended her life, she would've wanted Charlie to enjoy herself.

In the main hall, vendors filled the space, calling out to attendees, hoping to make sales. She stared at the crowd. The first panel she wanted to see didn't start for another half hour, so she had time to wander.

From behind her, she heard, "Hey, gorgeous."

Win. He came. Her heart swelled. She spun and her smile faltered. "Best. Hi."

He narrowed his eyes a fraction. "Expecting someone else?"

"No, not really. What are you up to?"

"No plans. Just thought I'd scope out the action." His gaze coasted over her body from the top of her head to the boots on her feet. "Who are you?"

She smiled and extended her hand. "Laura Nim, elven archer, from *The Order of Resskaar*."

He shook her hand and leaned into a half bow. "Laura Nim. Still using an anagram?"

"Of course."

As he straightened, he looked up in thought. "Still *Star Wars*?"

"Luminara, Jedi." She could've given him a

few more minutes and he would've figured it out. When they'd played together, they both used anagrams of *Star Wars* characters for their in-game personas. His mind could catalogue possibilities at an amazing speed.

"New hacker name, new RPG name. Anything else?"

She shrugged. Of course she'd changed over the last three years. Who hadn't?

"Why'd you stop using Punisher for hacking?"

Heat rose to her cheeks and she was glad for the paint. Jonah was the only person who knew her hacker name and why she'd chosen it. The vigilante comic book antihero seemed like a good idea at the time. "I was done being that person. It was time to move on."

He nodded as if he understood, but how could he? He'd left.

"So, now you're Rook?"

"Like the chess piece. The top part looks like a castle turret?" She pointed at herself as if he was slow. "Castle. Get it?"

"I get it. Just seemed too simple for you."

She gave him a slight shove. "I'm a simple girl, Best. Always have been."

"Not really." He said it without humor. There was heat and attraction in his eyes and something else she couldn't quite make out.

"I'm headed to a panel on creating dynamic gaming characters. Want to join me?" Charlie had no idea why she would invite him to spend more time with her. It was a huge mistake waiting to happen. Or maybe it already did. A brief hour ago she'd convinced herself she shouldn't be so easy.

"I was thinking about that one. Let's go." He took a step forward to walk side by side. "You feel okay after last night?"

"I'm good. I wasn't nearly as drunk as you thought I was."

"I know, but I wasn't taking any chances. When I take you to bed again, Charlie, you will be totally aware."

The low rumble of his voice tingled her nerves, and she covered with a haughty laugh. "Maybe that was your only shot and you blew it."

He leaned close and said, "We both know that's not true."

She took a sharp turn down the next hall and searched for the right room instead of responding to him. The simple statement should've angered her, but he was right. She'd wanted him last night. She'd want him again. This time, though, she would keep it simple. She'd spend time with him and enjoy the week escaping from her reality.

When she entered the conference room, a tall blue-painted man with bulging tattoos waved.

Leaving Jonah near the door, Charlie rushed ahead to say hi to Derek. He was a regular at this con. They'd met when she came the first time two years ago. He scooped her up and swung her in a big hug. "Hey, good to see you."

~

JONAH WATCHED AS SOME DUDE WHO COULD EASILY

be a bodyguard picked Charlie up like she was a toy. Her voice held real affection, unlike the overly friendly greeting he'd gotten from her in the lobby yesterday. The fake had worn off, though, and she was his Charlie again.

As she chatted with her friend, and Jonah chose to believe it was nothing more, he grabbed two seats for them near the back of the room. He sat and watched Charlie talk animatedly with the jolly blue giant.

When he'd caught her in the lobby, he hadn't expected to see her. In truth, he figured she'd be sleeping off her hangover. The words of greeting slipped from his mouth before he could censor them. The look on her face told him that she'd thought he was Win. He should've spilled it right there, but he feared that she would leave. That she wouldn't listen to why he'd been part of her life for more than a year without revealing himself.

It would all sound like bullshit. Even he knew that. Right now, all he wanted was to spend time with her, make sure she really was as okay as she said she was. And maybe see what they could be to each other now. He'd barely slept last night thinking about being with Charlie. She'd said she'd never regret him. He had no idea how much of that was the alcohol talking and how much she really meant, but it was an open door.

That was all he needed.

A guy at the front of the room tapped the microphone to begin. Jonah thought he'd lost Charlie to her friend, but as the moderator introduced the first speaker, Charlie slid into the chair next to him.

"Thanks for saving me a spot," she whispered.

"Any time."

They sat side by side as friends during the lecture. They laughed at the same jokes and listened to the criticisms of current games. Jonah listened to know what players wanted so he could improve their gaming experience. He didn't know why Charlie wanted in on this panel. Was this where she wanted to take her career?

As they wrapped up questions from the floor, Charlie nudged him. "I'm going to head out to grab some food before the next session. See you later?"

Although he wanted to hear the remaining answers, he found himself asking, "Can I join you?"

"Sure."

When they were back in the main hall, he reached for her hand to fight against the crowd. She didn't shy away from his touch, so even when the throng of people passed, he continued to hold on, running his thumb along her knuckles.

"Are you flirting with me?"

He stopped and yanked her over near the wall. Doing so made her body collide with his. "Of course I'm flirting with you. I want to kiss you again."

She tilted her head up. "What's stopping you, Best?

He lowered himself a little. "Why do you call me that?"

Her eyebrows furrowed. "It's your name?"

"My name is Jonah, but the only time you ever called me Jonah was in the bedroom."

She snorted. "It's a little presumptuous for you to think I should call you Best in the bedroom."

As much as he wanted a real answer, he couldn't stop the laugh. He loved her snarky humor, and although he'd heard it while playing *Resskaar*, nothing beat it in person.

When his laugh slowed, she leaned in and flicked her tongue on his earlobe. "I call you Best because you taught me a lot. Out here, with the games and the computers and the code, you are the best." Her breath whispered across his skin, making his pulse quicken. "But in the bedroom, it was just you and me. Everything else stripped away."

Damn, that was a good reason. Her pale blue eyes shone with honesty.

"How hungry are you?" His voice was strangled and it was her turn to laugh.

"Are you offering something better?"

"When's the next session you want to see?"

"A little over an hour."

"Let's go to my room."

Her smile broadened. "Mine's closer."

He yanked her again, plowing through the crowds and lines, shooting straight for the elevator. When the elevator doors closed, they were crammed in with about eight other people. Charlie pressed against his body.

He looked down to the V on her chest. "How far down does the paint go?"

She ground her hips against his. "You'll have to explore if you want to know."

Several pairs of eyes looked their way, as if other riders had hoped Jonah would peel away her clothes. Instead, he ran a finger across her waist where her vest met her pants. A simple strip of flesh, smooth against the pad of his finger. "I'm thinking not this far."

She bumped her hips again, and the bell dinged for her floor. They quietly excused themselves to get through the people and out the door. Their walk to her room was slower than the walk to the elevator had been mostly because Charlie walked backward in front of him, kissing his neck and tripping both of them as they made their way down the hall.

Charlie slid her key card in the slot and they tumbled through the door. The curtains were drawn, and only a sliver of light eked through at the edges. Charlie pulled him deeper into the room. She backed away, and he heard the popping sound of snaps being unfastened.

"Wait," he said and slid his hand along the wall searching for a light switch. With a quick flick, the bedside lamp glowed, and he saw that Charlie had her vest open.

The blue paint made a wobbly V down the center of her chest. She wasn't wearing a bra and the sides of the vest clung to her breasts. He flipped the vest aside, and she let it slide down her arms and drop to the floor.

She looked down at her skin. A low chuckled sounded. "Maybe I should shower first."

"No. I can't wait, and all the good parts have no paint." He lowered his mouth to her nipple and sucked. When the peak stiffened, he moved to the other breast and repeated the action. The sway of her hips demanded he move faster. He kissed his way down her torso and opened the pants. He slid them down her legs, pausing to take note of the fact she wasn't wearing any underwear.

He planted a wet kiss at the top of her trimmed mound, which earned him a groan. The scent of her arousal made him hard. Pushing her to sit on the bed, Jonah knelt on the floor and removed her boots and then her pants.

Charlie leaned back on her elbows and watched his every move. "You know, you could speed this up a little. I might still want to have lunch before the next panel."

"It's been a long time. I'm in no hurry." His dick definitely disagreed with his mouth. She looked bizarre with her pointy ears, blue face and arms, and pale white skin everywhere else.

She hopped up on her knees on the bed and yanked his shirt over his head. He toed off his gym shoes and pushed her back onto the bed.

He lowered his face to hers and kissed her as he moved his hand lower. "This paint tastes awful."

She giggled. "I told you I'd take a shower."

But then she raised her hips to meet his hand, and he forgot about kissing her and the taste of paint. She was wet and slick, and when his fingers rubbed over her clit, she moaned. Jonah picked up the pace of his hand, watching the quick rise and fall of her breasts. He lowered his head and sucked a nipple into his mouth.

Charlie threaded her fingers into his hair and held him as she rode his hand. He couldn't wait anymore. He hadn't been in a hurry, but now, seeing Charlie naked, wanting him, he couldn't wait. He pulled away. Although Charlie didn't say anything, she shot him a dirty look. He took off his jeans and grabbed the condom from his pocket.

He slid the condom on and then slid into her. Her breath hitched as he pushed deeper, but then she sighed against him. She was hot and slick, and he wanted to enjoy the sensation for a minute, but Charlie started to buck against him and he lost all rational thought. He began pumping into her, and he felt like a teenager not quite in control.

Hadn't Charlie always made him feel that way?

His balls tightened before he registered the feeling and he stopped. He needed to slow down, let her catch up. He rested his forehead against her shoulder and began to do math equations in his head.

Charlie leaned up and whispered in a husky voice, "Deep and hard, Jonah. Just the way I like it."

She squeezed around him, and no amount of calculus would save him. He drove into her mindlessly until he exploded. His muscles tensed and then he groaned with release. He lay against her, panting. Moments passed. Sweat ran off his forehead, and he registered that Charlie was breathing heavily.

But she hadn't come. Fuck, he felt like a shit. He thought he was going to make something right between them, but he got her into bed and just ended up satisfying himself. He was an ass.

He slowly lifted off her, determined to get her off.

As he pulled out of her, she began laughing. Not a satisfied *fuck yeah, that was great* laugh. Not a *you touched me and I'm ticklish* laugh. This was a *you're a ridiculous lover* laugh.

Jonah braced an elbow next to Charlie's head. "I know I said I wasn't in a hurry, but you do things to me, Charlie. I'll get you there. No need to laugh at me."

He tried to play it off like it was no big deal, but what man wanted to be laughed at in bed?

She was laughing so hard, tears trickled down her cheeks, and she couldn't catch her breath. She shook her head and grabbed his wrist.

Great. Now he wouldn't even have the chance to redeem himself.

"Wait." The single word appeared to cost her all of her oxygen, but she didn't stop laughing.

Fuck this. He pushed up and away from her.

She took a slow, steadying breath. "Jonah."

"I get it, Charlie." He closed his eyes because he was embarrassed and pissed off. This was not how things were supposed to go.

"No, you don't." She rose on her knees again and brushed her fingers over his chest.

It took a minute, but he realized she wasn't trying to turn him on. She was tracing something on him. He opened his eyes and looked down at her. She used his chest like a damn canvas and finger painted on him. The stupid body paint had rubbed off her and onto him.

"This was why I laughed. It had nothing to do with your performance."

He wished he could believe that. He pulled off the condom and turned toward the bathroom. When the door clicked closed, he looked in the mirror. He did look pretty ridiculous. Blue-green smudges marked his nose, cheek, and chest. Then he noticed what Charlie had traced. She wrote "Thank you."

And of course, she'd written in backward so that it appeared the right way in the mirror.

He laughed and grabbed a washcloth to clean up.

CHAPTER FIVE

$\mathcal{A}$s soon as the bathroom door clicked shut, Charlie got out of bed. She redressed and fixed her body paint. The whole situation would've been better had she taken a shower like she'd suggested. But no, the man who wasn't in a hurry turned out to be in a bigger hurry than she'd been in.

Not that she'd hold it against Jonah. Not much anyway. Their encounter, as brief as it was, had been the best time she'd had in longer than she could remember.

Definitely better than anything she'd shared with her ex, Ethan. The only thing better was her relationship with an imaginary dwarf.

God, her life was sad.

The bathroom door opened and Jonah stepped out. Why his nakedness surprised her she couldn't say, but she loved looking at him. She allowed her gaze a slow wander up his body, fit but not muscle-bound. When she reached his face, she didn't like the expression.

"Why are you dressed?"

"Let's face it. The moment passed. And I'm still hungry for lunch."

"No fucking way. I deserve the chance to redeem myself." He stepped closer and pulled her to his body. "You *know* I'm better than that."

She laughed again. Hell, yeah, she knew how good he was, but she wouldn't give him the satisfaction of admitting it. She patted his bare chest. "Everyone's entitled to an off day."

"An off moment. I'm not done."

She sobered. "Really, Jonah. It's fine. More than fine."

He studied her face and then pointed to his chest. "Why *thank you*? I know you didn't get off like I did."

She sighed. "Even without the earth-shattering orgasm that we both know you're capable of delivering, you gave me an awesome time. I haven't had that much fun in forever." Remembering Sylvie and Kraven, she added, "I needed fun."

"I can make it even better." His hand stroked across her back.

"As tempting as that is, I spent more than I can afford to get to this con. I'm not spending the entire time in bed with you." Although a few more hours would suit her just fine, she couldn't afford to make any assumptions about what this was between them. "Get dressed and I'll let you buy me lunch."

He rolled his eyes, but turned to the bed where his clothes lay scattered. She didn't move from her position but watched as he bent over. Exceptional view.

She loved the ease of everything with Jonah. No pretense, no pretending to be anything but what she was.

Which was a cold hard reminder that who she was hadn't been enough for him and he'd left. This time, she was prepared. She knew they only had a few short days and she'd enjoy them. Having sex with Jonah was always enjoyable. She'd hack and play and learn. Maybe she could even tap him for some networking help to find a real job.

But then she'd have to admit to him that she'd dropped out of school, and she wasn't ready to do that.

With his jeans tugged back on, Jonah turned to face her with his shirt in hand and just smiled. "You sure you don't want to skip lunch?"

"If we skip lunch, we're also going to skip the afternoon sessions. I want to get my money's worth." She grabbed her bow and arrows and slung them over her shoulder as he finished getting dressed. If this had happened at any other time or place, she would've taken him up on his offer. But this wouldn't have happened at any other time or place. It was a fluke that they ran into each other here. Jonah hated cons.

They walked out the door together, Charlie feeling pretty damn relaxed and confident. In the hall, Jonah put his arm around her and said, "I don't know what you're smiling about. I'm the one who has the reason to be grinning."

She bumped him with her hip. "I'm getting a free lunch. Plus, I know you well enough to know that you'll make it up to me. You don't like owing anyone, and you'll feel like you owe me."

"I plan to pay back with interest."

A shiver of anticipation shot up Charlie's back. Her week was definitely looking up.

THEY ATE LUNCH TOGETHER, AND CHARLIE couldn't believe the comfort level she'd felt with Jonah. Having lunch with an ex, especially right after having some mediocre sex, should be weird. He managed to make it not weird. As long as she pushed away thoughts about how and why he'd left years ago, she had a good time, like being with an old friend, instead of the guy who had left her.

After finishing off her overpriced cheeseburger and fries, Charlie stood and patted her stomach. "Thanks for the meal. That made up for skipping breakfast."

"No problem. I probably owe you dinner too. Are you free later?"

She took the question for what it really was—a fishing expedition. She wasn't sure how honest she wanted to be with him. Reveal that she had no plans with anyone else? How desperate would that make her sound?

"As you know, I have the hackfest later, but I could probably be available for an early dinner or a late drink." A sudden thought struck her. "Don't you think it might cause problems being with me?"

"How so?" He dropped cash on the table for a tip, a generous one at that, and signed the bill to his room.

"Fraternizing with a contestant might be misconstrued as cheating. Especially if I win."

The smirk on his face said plenty. He didn't think she had a shot at winning. "I told you before. A third party planned the challenges. I don't know what they are until we're all in the room together."

She bit down the urge to smack him and call him on his lack of faith in her abilities. He wasn't her boyfriend anymore. She had no reason to expect his support. "But everyone else doesn't know that."

"Let me worry about it. Where are you going next?"

She checked her schedule. "There's a panel about harassment in fandom and then I'm on to a discussion about all things Joss Whedon. After that, I'm not sure. How about you?"

They made their way through the restaurant, non-con-goers still looking at Charlie like she was an alien. She would've thought they'd be used to the costumes by now.

"At the risk of sounding like I'm stalking you, I planned to attend the harassment panel. It's a work thing. We've had some instances of harassment in the forums and occasionally in game. It bothers me that people who want to play are afraid to."

She thought of Kraven and what happened last night. "What can you do about it if it's happening in game? It is what it is. It's the in-person shit that makes me crazy."

"Was that the reason for your military wear to the hackfest yesterday?"

She nodded. "I haven't participated in too many live competitions, but for the few I've been exposed to, guys are assholes." She paused. "No offense."

He laughed. "Saying 'no offense' doesn't make it okay."

She lifted a shoulder. "I know. I don't care if it's okay. It's not okay for guys to treat me like shit and say insulting, vulgar things just because I'm a woman."

"Chill. I wasn't implying that it is okay. And there are plenty of assholes out there. I've had to boot a bunch from *Resskaar* for their behavior. But those of us who aren't assholes enjoy having women in the game."

She thought of Win and knew that to be true. They walked into the conference room, which was actually one of the banquet halls. The convention organizers obviously thought this was going to be a big draw. She looked at the attendees and rechecked her watch. The session was due to start in three minutes.

The room was half empty and the audience was almost all women. Her hopes for engaging in meaningful conversation fell.

Jonah walked up a couple of rows and said, "Something wrong?"

"Hell, yeah. Look around. What's the purpose of this panel if the entire audience is women? We're the ones being harassed. It's preaching to the choir."

He scanned the room. "True, but their stories are important. The panelists and some of the guests are listening. They—we—want to improve the gaming experience for everyone. If we don't know what you want, how can we fix it?"

Yeah, Jonah had a point, he always did, but the conversation was going to feel hollow and she knew that.

JONAH KNEW CHARLIE WAS READY TO BOLT. SHE never wanted to do anything that might be a waste of time. She looked at this audience and saw a waste of time. He wished she could open up a little and let things play out just to see what might happen. The moderator tapped the mike and as she began introductions for the panelists, more people claimed seats. Still mostly women, but the room filled a bit more.

He listened to the bios of the speakers. They were a group of tech specialists, software developers, and security analysts. Then there was an author and a convention organizer. They each gave a brief speech about what they hoped to get out of the discussion, and then they opened the floor to questions and comments.

Charlie was right in that nothing would change because of this one panel, but this discussion was an eye-opener for him. He'd known about harassment, had seen it firsthand, but he didn't really know what it did to the victims until he heard their stories.

As each woman stood and explained what had happened to her and how she felt, Charlie nodded or grunted her assent. She shifted in her seat, crossing and uncrossing her legs and arms. When they called for last comments, she shot out of her chair and rushed to the microphone.

Jonah was stunned. He hadn't expected Charlie to speak up. He leaned forward and watched her body language as closely as he listened to her words.

"Like the rest of you, I've experienced the minor harassment when players realize I'm a woman. From the taunts of 'girls can't play' to being told that I must be an ugly, fat bitch that no real man would want. We're all used to that. I think most of us ignore it and let it roll off. But we can't. Dismissing it allows it to continue as something that's not only acceptable, but expected."

She paused and looked over her shoulder at him. He wished he knew what he could do to offer her reassurance.

She turned back to the mike. "Last night, while playing my favorite game, another character who was angry at me attacked me." She took a deep breath. "He ripped off my clothes, and he planned to rape me—my character. This game has been my refuge, my safe place to relax and explore, but he took some of that from me last night."

Jonah stiffened. He shouldn't have left her in game alone. He should've stayed online to make sure she was okay.

"The thing is, as a player, I can only do so much to keep myself and my identity safe. It's up to you"—she pointed at the panelists—"to keep my player safe. Why was this cretin allowed to rip off my clothes? In what universe would that ever be acceptable?"

Now she turned back, and the look she shot at Jonah was full of accusation.

"The developers, the security analysts, the businesses who take my hard earned money should never have allowed that to happen."

She walked away from the mike and kept walking until she hit the door. The room was silent. Jonah rose as the moderator began to speak to the panelists. He pushed open the door and looked around for Charlie, but he couldn't see her. As easy as it should've been to spot a blue-green elf walking around with a bow and arrows, it wasn't. The sea of Klingons and stormtroopers swallowed her up.

Although she moved quickly, he knew where to find her. No matter how angry or hurt she might be about sharing that story, she wouldn't miss a chance to be with other Browncoats. Three years ago, they'd spent a weekend lying in bed watching the entire *Firefly* series. Jonah considered himself lucky Charlie loved that instead of *Buffy the Vampire Slayer*. He snagged a schedule to find the Joss Whedon discussion. It didn't start for at least another twenty minutes, so he went in search of some coffee before tracking down Charlie.

The long lines for coffee had him getting to the next session with only five minutes to spare. The Whedonites filled the hall, so Charlie should stand out in this crowd. He glanced through the groups, hoping she wasn't hiding from him, regretting that she'd told him her plans for the afternoon.

Then he saw her. She didn't appear to still be angry. Her gait was smooth, and she chatted with a guy dressed in a leather costume covered in metal studs. Jonah had no idea who he was supposed to be. Charlie pulled up short when she noticed him.

"I brought you a coffee. Got a minute?"

She raised an eyebrow but took the cup. "I refuse to be late for this session, so talk fast."

"What happened in game last night. Was it the first time something like that happened?"

She pulled back a little. "You mean you aren't even going to question *if* it really happened?"

Of course he wouldn't, he'd seen it, but he couldn't let her know.

"Why wouldn't I believe you?"

She shook her head. "Yes, it was the first, and I hope last, time."

"We've had some issues with hackers going in and changing code to cheat the game. Usually harmless stuff. I don't know how this guy was able to do that. You have to believe that I would never work on a game that would allow that to happen to a player."

She sipped from her coffee, and a smile flickered on her face. "You remembered how I like my coffee?"

The doors to the conference room opened, and people shuffled in and out. Charlie stepped toward the flock moving in, and Jonah grabbed her elbow. In her ear, he whispered, "I remember how you like everything. See you later."

He released her elbow and backed away from the crowd going in. They more or less pushed Charlie into the room, but she looked back at him with a stunned look.

What, did she think that just because he left town, he'd forgotten her?

That wasn't even in the realm of possibilities.

Jonah walked back to his room to make plans for his date with Charlie. They'd left it open-ended so instead of planning dinner before the hackfest, he decided a late-night dessert would be better. Then he could convince her to spend the night with him.

He also made some notes about the session on harassment and checked in with Tim to see if the team had figured out how Kraven had managed the modification.

The more he thought about the issues facing female gamers, the more he thought about how to change the culture. But he was one guy. How could he affect a sea of change?

CHAPTER SIX

Charlie left the Whedon session feeling rejuvenated. She loved being around people who understood her. While her friends accepted her, they didn't really get her love of gaming and sci-fi. They didn't even know about her hacking. Now that Layla was going to work for the NSA, Charlie wouldn't be able to tell her at all. There was probably some law that said Layla would have to arrest her or some shit.

But here, in crowds of fans, she felt not only comfortable, but at home. Among the freaks and weirdos.

And then there was Jonah. She didn't know how he fit into anything, but she was just as comfortable around him as she was the cosplayers. She made some fast friends in the Whedon session, and they were all heading to the bar for a drink. She'd also promised Derek they'd get together for a drink. She pulled out her phone and shot a quick text to Derek to let him know where she'd be in case he wanted to join.

Jake, a guy dressed as a hobbit, touched her shoulder. "So tell me about this game, *The Order of Resskaar*. I've never heard of it, but it sounds like it might be worth a try."

Charlie couldn't tell if he was really interested or if he was using the game as a way to flirt. That was one thing she noticed with guys at this con. Many of them were shy, geeky guys, but here, they gained confidence and talked. She couldn't imagine Jake ever approaching her in a regular bar.

"It's still a small world comparatively. It's been out for a couple of years, but it's growing. The basic premise is that Resskaar has been captured by Jek-Solared. The individual guilds have missions to complete in order to save Resskaar and restore order. While in captivity, Resskaar is able to get messages out to aid you in your mission. Then there's the usual pillaging and fighting that goes along with everything." They walked into the bar as she finished her explanation, and as she drifted toward a table, she half expected Jake to find his group of friends.

"How long have you been playing?"

"Almost since the beginning. About two years." She looked around to see if Derek had arrived and to get the attention of a waitress.

"What do you want? I'll go to the bar and grab it."

"A light beer would be great. Thanks."

Jake went to order, and a couple of women that she'd seen in the last session waved and asked if they could join her table.

"Uh, sure, but leave a chair for Jake. He went to go grab some drinks."

"Oh, Jake." The woman had a grin on her face, and Charlie couldn't figure out if it was a look of teasing or fondness.

"Is there something I should know?"

"Don't let him fool you. He acts all shy and reserved, but he's all alpha, if you know what I mean."

No, Charlie had no idea where this conversation was headed. "We're just talking about gaming. Nothing else."

"That's how it always starts out. Jake finds a girl every year. Singles her out. Makes her feel special. And then *wham!* He moves in."

"Are you saying this guy is dangerous?"

She laughed loud and hard. Her friend joined in. "No. He just leaves you so unsuspecting. By the time he works his magic, you're into him."

"No, I'm not. I'm not looking to hook up with anyone." Except Jonah. Or Win. Shit, she really wished she could've convinced Win to make the trip to the con.

"Then you really don't know what you're missing."

Charlie leaned forward on the table. "Are you telling me that you and Jake...?"

"Last year." Her smile widened.

Her friend sat forward. "Two years ago."

"Wait." Charlie couldn't believe this. "You mean you each hooked up with Jake?"

The first woman laughed again. "Sue was the

one who told me about him, made sure we crossed paths."

Sue touched Charlie's arm. "He's a great way to spend your nights."

"My nights are already booked."

"Are you sure?" Sue glanced over her shoulder where Jake was headed back toward them. "Because Jen and I might be able to convince him that once wasn't enough."

"Uh, yeah. All yours. I was just having a friendly conversation." Jake had gotten waylaid by another guy, and Charlie had to ask. "Isn't it weird knowing you and your friend have been with the same guy? Won't there be some awkwardness when he gets back here?"

"No. That's the best thing about Jake. It is what it is. A good time, a few laughs. Everyone leaves satisfied and happy."

Jake set a beer in front of Charlie. Not wanting to let on to the wealth of information that she'd received, Charlie pointed to the women. "Jake, this is Sue and Jen."

"Oh, we've met," Sue purred. "You remember us, don't you, Jake?"

"Of course." He bent over and kissed Sue's cheek and then did the same to Jen. "Do you ladies need another drink?"

"No, we're good."

Jake settled in the chair between the two women, and Charlie couldn't quite decide if she should be offended. They weren't on a date or anything, and she wasn't even interested in Jake, but watching him sit between two women who were so obviously into him bugged her. Luckily, she didn't have to suffer through it too long because Derek walked through the door. Thank God he was built like a brick wall. He was easy to spot.

"Excuse me, guys. I see a friend I've been looking for. Jake, it was good to meet you. Thanks for the beer. Sue, Jen, have a great time." She stepped away from the table without waiting for a response.

"Derek," she called, and the big man turned.

"Hey, glad you texted. Let me grab a beer. You need one?"

She glanced at her still full bottle. "Sure."

She followed Derek to the bar, and they took seats there.

Over the next hour they chatted about everything from gaming to hacking. Jake and company had been pleasant enough, but hanging with Derek was fun. She was sorry to have to pull away from him, but she needed to shower before the hackfest. No way would she show up in costume for that. Competition would be difficult enough without the inevitable snickers and teasing.

She said her good-bye to Derek with the promise that they'd meet up again before the end of the con and headed back to her room. The dark room felt lonely compared to the rest of the crowded hotel where she could find someone to talk to. She shook her head and her morose thoughts. Spending time alone was normal. It shouldn't bother her now.

Scrubbing off the body paint took longer than

she expected, especially since it seemed to come off so readily against Jonah. Thinking of his paint-smeared body turned her on, and she thought about satisfying that need before the competition, but decided to wait until after, when Jonah would be available for her satisfaction. He'd said he planned to make it up to her. With interest.

Charlie pulled on the baggy cargo pants and sweatshirt and pulled her hair back. If anyone gave her more than a passing glance, they would realize she was female, but she was too tired to do more. And she shouldn't have to disguise herself. She'd made it through the first round just like everyone else.

She grabbed her bag and went in search of caffeine. By the time she got to the conference room, many of the seats were filled. She'd never known such a prompt group of hackers before. Jonah was at the front of the room in a quiet conversation with the moderators. She took a seat and set up her laptop and drank her coffee. Being the second challenge, tonight would no doubt last longer than the night before. She eyed her competition. They could've been any of the guys she'd run into at meet-ups over the years. Some were too serious, like they were afraid that by conversing with someone they might reveal their secrets.

Jonah suddenly looked up as if someone had called him. As the moderator continued to talk, Jonah scanned the room. His gaze landed on her, and the heat in the stare made her squirm in her seat.

She didn't have time for lustful thoughts. She needed to focus.

~

Jonah knew Charlie came into the room because the air shifted. It wasn't a sexual thing—at least he chose to believe that. And he wasn't the only one to notice her. The rumblings of a couple of guys behind him verified that. Although they hadn't made any inappropriate comments, they were nudging each other and pointing at Charlie. She was one of only two women who made it to the second round. The other woman hadn't arrived yet, but Jonah hoped she would.

He checked the time. The challenge would start in less than five minutes, and a bunch of people still hadn't shown. It didn't surprise him. Many hackers came to competitions like this not knowing how tough it was going to be. Even though they made the first cut, some would've recognized that they didn't have what it takes to win.

Jonah made his way to the door to close it for the start, and three more people squeezed through, one being the other woman. They plopped into chairs and set up laptops while Carl, the moderator, read through directions.

Tonight's challenge was more difficult. Jonah wasn't sure how many would complete it, and he worried about Charlie. When he'd left three years ago, he'd seen natural ability in her, but she had a habit of rushing into things without thought.

Luckily for her, her gut instinct was usually on target. The challenge planned for tonight would require strategy. If the goals were reached out of order, the hacker would still finish, but not be able to win. Sequence counted here.

He perched on a stool near the door and drank from a bottle of water. The clacking of keys lulled him into a comfort zone. It was kind of like being at work. He zoned out, thinking about Kraven. Tim still hadn't found how the guy had gotten in to change the code, but the altered code had been discovered and changed back.

Tim put someone else on blocking Kraven's account so he could focus on the security aspects. Jonah exhibited extreme restraint by not finding out who Kraven really was and paying him a visit in person. Attacking Charlie had been bad enough, but this asshole had done it in Jonah's game.

Thinking about the game brought him back to thinking about Charlie. He needed to tell her he was Win, but he didn't know how. Things were strange between them. He shouldn't have slept with her without coming clean, but all he could think about was getting her naked again. If he told her his online identity, that option would be out the window.

To get images of a naked Charlie out of his mind, he strolled the room to watch the hackers work and see how they approached the challenge. In addition to finding a way past firewalls, they were expected to leave a nugget, their own personal calling card as proof they were there. An hour in, a guy jumped up and said, "What the fuck?"

Other hackers barely looked up from their screens. This group was focused. Both Jonah and Carl went to see what the problem was.

"I'm almost halfway through, and I backtracked to make sure I didn't miss anything. Someone deleted my trail."

"Everybody freeze." A few more keystrokes clicked. "Hands up. Now!" Carl's bellow broke them from their concentration. "The rules clearly state that you can't interfere with another player's action. Doing so qualifies for immediate dismissal."

Jonah watched the room while Carl talked. He hoped it wasn't Charlie who had cheated. He quickly dismissed the idea. Charlie was always honorable. She wouldn't cheat.

Carl studied each player. "Anyone want to come clean?"

"Hell, no, they won't. Why would they? I'm ahead of everyone. They take me out, they can win."

"Take a seat." Carl pointed and Jonah followed. In a low voice, he said, "We didn't plan for this. How do you want to handle it? We figured the threat would be enough."

"Give me a minute. I'll get in and see if I can figure out who did it." Jonah walked to the front of the room where Carl had his laptop set up. Jonah felt all eyes on him. He was glad he wouldn't have to figure out the path to take since Carl had it all outlined. Jonah logged on and began reading code. On the first three sites, the same players marked their path. Charlie was one of them. He held back his smile. He wasn't supposed to have favorites.

He jumped ahead a few sites. Poison, the hacker who was pissed off, disappeared at the seventh site. When Jonah went further ahead, he could see Poison logged on the eleventh site. It was possible that Poison got sidetracked and took the wrong path, but not likely. The guy was good.

Jonah eased back out and looked for the changes that might reveal the cheater. The hackers were getting restless, and they began popping open cans of energy drinks. From the corner of his eye, he saw Charlie stand and walk over to Carl. Then she left.

He knew she wasn't guilty. Plus, she hadn't taken her stuff. He needed to ignore her. Carl came over a minute later and slid a piece of paper next to the keyboard. MAVERICK.

Jonah looked at Carl who shrugged. Following a lead, even if it was unsubstantiated, had to be better than following each of the more than twenty players in the room. Jonah looked at Maverick's progress. Sure enough, he had been on Poison's heels through the eighth site. Then there was a lapse of fifteen minutes before he appeared on the ninth site.

After looking at the code and checking out Maverick's patterns, Jonah saw it. The trail that had been deleted that showed Maverick had been there and then exited without leaving his mark.

There was no reason to do that unless you didn't want people to know you'd arrived.

Carl straightened. "Maverick." Everyone shifted as Charlie reentered the room. "Are you really going to make me pull registration to match names with ID? Grow the hell up."

A guy in the corner shoved away from the table. "I'm Maverick."

Carl tilted his head to get Maverick to come forward.

"Screw this." Maverick grabbed his laptop and stormed out, not even waiting to hear the accusation.

Carl took a deep breath and said to Poison, "I'm not sure how to make this fair for you."

"Don't worry about me. As long as no one else fucks with me, I'll smoke everyone in the room."

When everyone quieted, Jonah stood. "I hope that's the last problem we run into. You guys have to realize that there's more to this competition than the prize money and ticket to Def Con. There are companies here looking for people like you. We want to hire brilliant thinkers. Not cheaters."

He walked away, disappointed because Maverick had been on his list of people to check out. Carl reclaimed his spot at the front of the room and announced time for players to restart. When they were all attacking their laptops, Carl wandered around before making his way back to Jonah.

When he was close, Jonah whispered, "Who gave you the tip?"

Carl looked over his shoulder. "The blonde. She sat there for five minutes, and you could tell something was poking her. I thought maybe she was the guilty one until she tucked that paper in my hand. Even then, I thought maybe she was trying to throw you off her trail."

The energy of the room buzzed. The sugar- and caffeine-fueled participants continued on their quest, but they were somber, like they just realized the rules were there for a purpose. Some stole glances at him, probably wondering who he was.

Not Charlie. She tapped away at keys, and he itched to check to see how far along she was. He couldn't wait until after this challenge. He wanted to know how she knew Maverick was guilty. She hadn't been sitting by him, so she couldn't have watched.

Because of the level of difficulty in this challenge, people stayed put when they finished. They needed to make sure they hadn't taken a wrong turn. Carl had also told them that the last challenge was going to be different and they needed to hang around for directions. Carl and Jonah hunkered down to check paths and code as people declared they'd reached the end.

Charlie was the third to finish. Jonah made sure that Carl checked her. Although he wouldn't cheat for her, he didn't want to take any chances with someone accusing him of letting her win. After they checked everything and announced the top ten finalists, the losers left.

Carl stood. "Tomorrow night, plan for what

might be an all-nighter. You'll need a partner because we'll be doing a capture the flag."

All ten hackers started mumbling, but Poison spoke up first. "What does that mean for the prize money and the Def Con registration?"

Carl smiled. "Glad you asked. We've got a second registration set, but you'll have to split the prize money. Still not a bad deal."

"What if we prefer to work alone?"

"The sponsors want to see how everyone works as part of a team." Carl didn't expand on that explanation, but Jonah could see that a few guys were not pleased by the prospect.

Jonah could've called it. Poison was a lone wolf. He wanted to do his own thing and not have to answer to anyone. He was skilled, Jonah would give him that, but he was arrogant.

The players all started looking around sizing each other up more than they had upon entering the room for the past two nights.

"You have until tomorrow night to decide. You don't have to declare anything now. Go have a drink. Get to know each other. We'll have this room open at least an hour early if you want to meet here."

Jonah wished he had entered the competition just so he could partner with Charlie. It had been so long since he worked side by side with her. It would've been fun.

But he had the chance for a different kind of fun as soon as the room cleared. He stood by the door and answered questions as participants filtered out. When Charlie came past, he stood in front of her, blocking others' view, and tucked his room key in her jacket pocket. "Any questions?"

She flashed a ready smile. "Not at all. I think I've got this handled."

Yeah, she had him handled all right.

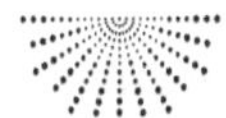

CHAPTER SEVEN

Charlie left the conference room feeling pretty damn good. Not only had she ranked in the top three, but Jonah was also keeping his word about getting together tonight. A key card in her pocket said plenty. The halls were quiet, as the vendors had wrapped up hours ago. She knew she'd find company in the bar if she wanted some.

What she really needed to do was figure out who she wanted to pair with for tomorrow's challenge. As she walked toward the elevator, she thought about the opposition. No way would she ask Poison; the dude was pretty toxic. She was sure he wouldn't want to work with her anyway; she was beneath him. Then again, he thought everyone was beneath him.

"Excuse me," someone behind her called.

Charlie turned around. The only other female in the hacking competition stared at her.

"Hi, I'm Jane. Uh, Cracker."

Charlie nodded. The name fit her. The girl

was as pale as a snowman. That probably wasn't why she'd chosen the hacker name, but Charlie wasn't looking to get into a lengthy conversation about the origins of their names. Jane continued to stare, so Charlie asked, "Can I do something for you?"

Jane shook her head as if to clear it. "Yeah, I was hoping you might want to pair up for tomorrow's challenge. You know, since we're the only two girls in the running."

"We should work together simply because we're the same sex?"

Color bloomed on Jane's cheeks. "Well, not the only reason. Obviously, we're both good. I mean, I get that you're better than me since you came in third, but you know what it's like with the guys. Most of them can't believe we're allowed in the same room. As if we're not worthy."

Of course Charlie knew.

"You don't really want to go through having to talk to all of the guys and hope one of them will partner with you, do you?"

"I also don't want to rush into an arrangement without considering all my options."

"Fair enough. Maybe we can grab a coffee tomorrow afternoon?"

"Sure. I'll look for you on the con floor. Have a good night." The elevator opened, and Charlie sincerely hoped Jane wouldn't follow. She wanted to go to her room and grab some clothes and then go to Jonah's room. Would spending the night interfere with her keeping it simple? Worse, was she being presumptuous to think she could spend the night in Jonah's room?

She rolled her eyes. She and Jonah had spent plenty of nights together, and he never had a problem with it before. A quick run through her room and then she went up two floors to Jonah's room. Part of her wished she had something special to wear, but she didn't even own any sexy lingerie.

All this thinking was making her nuts. This was Jonah. He liked her the way she was. At least while she was naked. She wasn't quite sure what else to think of Jonah. She'd never gotten around to asking why he left without a word. Mostly she was afraid of the answer. He'd moved onto bigger and better things.

And she'd needed to grow up.

Which she had done. Could they have some kind of future now? Charlie couldn't even go there. Once in Jonah's room, she took out her laptop and logged in to *Resskaar*. She hadn't returned since the whole ugly scene with Kraven. A bit of guilt tugged at her when she realized that part of why she logged on was to see if Win was around. She missed hanging with him.

The game opened, and she saw herself on the floor of the house where Kraven had attacked her. She ran from the room and back through the forest to her cave. Win would look for her there. Once she was away from the house, she took a moment to look at stats. Win wasn't logged in now. Neither was Kraven, thank God. But there was no sign that Win had been on since he'd saved her. No missions completed.

He hadn't even left her a message.

That wasn't like Win. He always talked to her after a big battle, and this had been way worse than any battle she'd faced. This was personal. Maybe that's why Win hadn't been around. What do you say to a friend who'd almost been raped?

She heard the quiet click of the room lock and looked up as Jonah came in.

"You're here," he said with a smile.

"Isn't this where you wanted me?"

"Actually, I want you naked in my bed, but I'll settle for this." He tossed his stuff on the table behind her laptop. "What are you doing?"

"I logged in to play *Resskaar* while I waited for you. Want to play? Talk nice to me and I might let you in my guild." She wagged her eyebrows and then winked.

A strange look crossed his face, but his smile held as he closed her laptop. "I'm not looking to play those kind of games tonight."

Her blood warmed as he spoke and edged closer to her. He grabbed her hand and tugged her to stand. "These are some seriously ugly clothes. I get you don't want to go ultra-feminine while hacking, but this is ridiculous."

He pulled her jacket off and then ran his fingers through her hair. She didn't move. Having his hands on her in any way made her blood rush. She'd missed this. A guy she really liked and cared for, one who would look into her eyes to turn her on.

"Much better," he mumbled and lowered his lips to hers.

The kiss was slow and sweet. Jonah took his time reacquainting himself with her mouth. They hadn't kissed earlier because of her body paint, and she hadn't thought it mattered. She was wrong. His kiss was a precursor to everything. He just kept kissing her as if there was nothing else.

Impatience propelled her forward, and she shoved him toward the bed. She was only able to move him because she'd caught him off guard. She felt his smile against her mouth a second before he planted his feet.

His mouth moved across her jaw and to her neck. Into her ear, he whispered, "I have a lot to make up for this morning and we have all night."

She shivered at the thought of all night. She tugged at his shirt and yanked until he stepped back far enough for her to pull it over his head. Then she followed with her shirt. Jonah moved slowly when he wasn't distracted. Charlie planned to do everything in her power to distract him; slow wasn't going to work for her. Before he moved in again, she whipped off her bra.

He groaned and Charlie knew she was on the right track. Jonah's hands became very busy with her breasts, so she was able to shift closer to the bed. Only a few more feet and she'd be able to push him down. She wasn't in the mood for games. She wanted Jonah naked.

Jonah unbuttoned her jeans as he kissed across her collarbone. The move grabbed her attention, so she stopped moving and just enjoyed the sensation. His hands slid into her pants and grabbed her ass, pushing her tight against him. She felt the hard length of his cock and gave his shoulders a shove.

The movement startled him enough that he stared at her with wide eyes.

"Get naked, Jonah." She pushed her jeans off and stepped out of them. He did the same. His dick sprang when he removed his underwear, and she licked her lips.

"Don't even think about it."

She raised an eyebrow.

"I mean, save it for later. I need to improve my reputation."

She laughed. "You're such a guy sometimes."

"Uh, all the time, thanks."

"No, I mean, you're worried about what? The fact that you didn't make me come this morning? It was still good sex. And it was fun."

"I don't know who's been telling you lies, but sex without an orgasm isn't good. I plan to show you good. Excellent even." He grabbed her waist, turned, and tossed her on the bed.

She liked Jonah when he was aggressive and pushy. He was so laid-back the rest of the time, it was a turn-on to know he only did this with her— in bed. She didn't want to stop to think if he was like this with other women.

And a second later, she couldn't think at all because Jonah's mouth was on her nipple, his fingers rubbing her clit. Then he slipped a finger in. Her hips caught his rhythm and met his hand. A second finger joined the first, and he curled them inside her while his thumb continued to stroke her clit.

It felt like her whole body was lifting off the bed, but his weight kept her grounded. He kissed her neck, her ear, and then back to her mouth. His hand picked up the pace, and her muscles convulsed as the orgasm washed over her. She was breathless, but Jonah continued to kiss her, stealing her oxygen, making her light-headed.

When her hips stopped moving, he levered himself above her, brought his fingers to his mouth, and licked them. "Tasty."

Then his tongue replaced his hand and he began to lap at her in slow, smooth strokes. Charlie was going to push him away. She was too sensitive, but as his tongue slid over and around her lips, everywhere but her clit, she felt her lust building again. He pushed his tongue into her, and a moan of approval vibrated against her.

Before she knew it, she gripped his hair and held him in place while he tasted and licked her. The need built slow and steady. Her breath began to hitch, and she tried to drag his mouth back to her clit, to give her the release she sought again, but he held fast. He would swipe his tongue close, circle around, but not quite hit the mark.

If this had been their first time, Charlie would've thought he needed a road map. But he was doing this intentionally. He was doing his best to torture her. He'd tongue fuck her for a minute or two and then pull away and nibble on the tendon at the juncture where her thigh met her pelvis.

Just when she thought the frustration would make her scream, Jonah came at her again, giving her a real reason to scream. He licked all over and finally sucked her clit into his mouth and held it between his teeth. She shattered after she screamed, and she couldn't breathe.

When she opened her eyes, Jonah's face was above hers with a satisfied grin. "Excellent?"

She couldn't talk; her lungs still couldn't fill to capacity, so she nodded.

He leaned close to her ear and whispered, "And I'm still not done with you, Charlie."

She closed her eyes and swallowed hard. She wasn't sure how much more she could take.

Jonah couldn't look in Charlie's eyes. When she was like this, she was so open and vulnerable. It made him feel like shit. But that didn't stop him from putting on a condom and sliding into her.

Being inside Charlie was like coming home. She hadn't been his first girlfriend, or his last, but she'd always been the only one he loved. Which was why he felt shitty for leaving her. Yet she accepted him back as if it had been no big deal.

He buried his face in her neck and breathed in her scent as he buried his cock as deep inside her as he could. She wrapped her legs around his hips and ran her fingers across his shoulders. He slowed his thrusts, but she bucked up against him.

"Faster."

He pulled away from the warmth of her body, and before he could make a move, she straightened her legs against his chest and hooked her ankles on his shoulders. He sank deep into her and moved faster to accommodate her request.

Their flesh slapped with the frenetic pace, and Charlie began to moan again, a sure sign that she wanted to come, that she was close. His hand slid down the front of her thigh, but her hand beat him to the mark. She began to rub herself, and the image was so fucking hot, he lost his last bit of concentration and felt his balls tighten. He dropped her legs and grabbed her shoulders, pounding into her as he emptied. Her hand was trapped between them. She came right after he started, her walls pulsing around him, milking him, pulling him closer. He pumped until he couldn't move anymore.

Then he collapsed.

Charlie slid her limbs away from him, but he wasn't ready to let go. His right arm remained beneath her as he rolled off. They both stared at the ceiling doing nothing but catching their breath.

Finally, she broke the silence. "I'll tell you, Best, that was beyond excellent."

He found the strength to push up on his elbow. He didn't want to read too much into her word choice, but even his ego needed stroking on occasion. "You are aware you just called me Best, right? There's no taking that back."

She winked at him. "I don't think I need to."

He laughed at the easy playfulness of their

conversation. "You make things too easy," he admitted.

Her face became serious, a flash of something in her eyes, but she pushed it away and smiled at him. "That's me, Easy Charlie."

"I didn't mean it like that. You know I didn't." He pushed hair off her forehead and stroked a finger down her cheek. "I mean this—talking, joking, laughing—I'm always comfortable with you. Easy like that."

The same brief look came back.

"What?" he asked.

She jumped up quickly, and he thought for a moment that she was going to leave. "Let's order room service. I'm starving."

One thing he should've remembered about Charlie was that she liked to eat, especially after having sex. He stretched out on the bed. "Go ahead. Order what you want. I'm going to shower and get some work done. You'll be here when I get out?"

She snickered. "You just offered me free food. Of course I'll be here."

He stood and wrapped a hand around the back of her neck to pull her close. "You might enjoy the food, but you're staying for the sex."

His mouth closed over hers before she could spout her snappy comeback. He kissed her breathless and then went to the bathroom. Yeah, he'd definitely missed Charlie. Now all he had to do was convince his boss that she was worth hiring.

CHAPTER EIGHT

Charlie inhaled a deep breath. Jonah knew how to short-circuit her brain. She'd wanted to ask why he'd left without a word, without a call. But he kept distracting her with fabulous kisses. Her mind clung to the idea about why she was here now, in his room.

They'd never had sexual compatibility issues and maybe that's all this was to Jonah. A great way to spend a weekend. With any other man, she could totally get behind that.

But Jonah was different. She needed to learn how to make him not different because when the weekend hit, Jonah was going to board a plane and leave her again.

She picked up the phone and ordered an obscenely large amount of food. She'd skipped dinner, and great sex always made her hungry. While she waited for the food to arrive, she grabbed Jonah's shirt and logged back in to *Resskaar*. She needed to talk to Win.

He still hadn't logged on and she was getting

worried. What if Kraven had gone after Win again?

When Jonah stepped out of the bathroom, a cloud of steam followed. He wore nothing, a testament to his level of comfort around her.

"Enjoying my shirt?"

"Much, thank you."

He crossed the room, kissed the top of her head, and asked, "The rush of sex is gone already, so you've turned back to the game? I'm wounded."

She laughed. They'd spent nights just like this three years ago. Sex, gaming, hacking. Laughing. When did it turn? When did it become too much for him?

The question was poised in her mouth as he pulled on his boxer briefs. She wanted to ask but thought better of it. Maybe there was such a thing as too much truth.

"Have you figured out how Kraven almost raped me?"

Charlie watched as the muscles in Jonah's back stiffened and bunched. When he turned around, his face was stone. "Not yet. We found the altered code and corrected it, but my team is still working on figuring out how he got in."

"I'm worried about my friend. He was there that night. He saved me, in fact, but he hasn't been back. I'm afraid that psycho did something to his character."

Jonah came back to her and squatted to put him at her eye level. His palm cradled her cheek. "The first thing we did was track that guy down and shut him out. He couldn't have done anything to your friend or anyone else. I promise you that."

His palm on her face warmed and comforted her. "But what if he just created a new profile, logged in another way? He's obviously got hacking skills."

"We followed his IP and flagged it. It'll hold him off while we figure out a long-term solution." His thumb stroked her cheekbone, just like he had while they were in bed talking. "Trust me, your friend is safe."

He spoke with such conviction that Charlie wanted to believe him, but hearing from Win was the only thing that would really set her mind at ease.

"Go ahead and play. I've got some work to catch up on." He took the seat opposite her at the small table and opened his laptop.

"Any secrets for *Resskaar* that you're working on? I'd love to beta a new version." She smiled and winked.

"I'll keep you in mind, but we have nothing ready just yet."

And then she lost him. His focus was on his screen. He was like a ninja on the keyboard. His strokes barely registered as clicks. Sometimes she'd woken in the middle of the night to find him typing away, but it was never the sound that disturbed her. It was feeling like he was gone, which he was every time he sat in front of a screen.

She turned back to her game and put on her headphones. Today, she wanted to hear people.

She wandered the woods. Her health and strength had returned, in large part due to Win. She checked her mission status and saw that three other members of her guild were on, so she went in search of them to see if they'd had contact with Win in the forums or outside the game.

As she approached the group, they rushed at her to talk about what had happened. How did they know about Kraven? She hadn't spoken to anyone since it happened.

Messages in the forums told them what had happened, and although no names were used, they figured it had been her. She told them how Win had saved her and asked if Win had been playing. Of course, she got the answer she'd been expecting, which was that no one had seen Win. Just as the disappointment sank in, a blink notified her of Win logging on.

A private message. *Meet me at the cave.*

She said quick good-byes to her guild and took off back in the direction she'd come from. As she burst through the trees, she saw him leaning nonchalantly against the mouth of the cave. "Hey, gorgeous."

His computerized voice made her heart leap. She rushed at him and jumped him. His arms circled her as his back smacked against the rock, her long body nearly twice the size of his toppling them. Good thing they were only pixels. In real life, that would hurt like a bitch.

Oh my God. Are you okay?

He set her down. "The real question is are you?"

I'm fine since I had a hero rescue me.

"And a fine rescue it was. It drained me of power." He paused. "And it freaked me out a bit. I've never seen anything like that."

Neither have I, but I have it on excellent authority that it won't ever happen again.

"Do I want to know who your authority is?"

Remember I asked you to come to this con because I ran into my ex?

"Sure."

He's a developer for the game.

"So you've gone and done something stupid because I wasn't there."

She smacked his shoulder. *Maybe. I'm not sure. The thing is, I feel so right when I'm with him. It's like it's too good to be true.*

"What's wrong with that?"

He's going to leave. Again.

"Maybe he won't if you ask him to stay."

Charlie hadn't thought of that, but she knew Jonah wouldn't stay. He had a life away from here. Plus, she had nothing to offer him. If she wanted someone like Jonah in her life, she needed to get her shit together.

Win waved a hand in front of her. "Did I lose you?"

No, just thinking.

He moved his body to look around her.

What are you looking for?

He laughed. "Smoke. I figure if you're thinking that hard, there's bound to be a fire."

You're a good friend. I really wish you would've come here. We would've had a blast together.

"I'm sure. I have to go. I work early. I just wanted to check on you to make sure you're okay."

I am. See you soon?

"Of course. I can't wait to get all the details about the con." Then he vanished.

What was with her and the disappearing acts of men in her life?

Seeing Win and knowing he was all right revitalized her, and she stormed back into the game, looking to do some fighting. She wouldn't be able to exact revenge on Kraven, but she'd be able to find plenty of other players to fit the bill. She glanced up quickly in time to see Jonah looking at her.

He smiled like he had a secret. She tossed her headphones on the table and leaned over to kiss him. She took a surreptitious peek at his screen. She didn't know what she thought she'd find, but it was rows of code, nothing exciting.

"What was that for?" he asked.

"Nothing. You were right. My friend is fine. I'm going to kick some ass now."

"Have fun." Then he went back to his screen.

As she put her headphones back on, she wondered what kind of secrets Jonah had.

THE ROOM SERVICE ARRIVED AND CHARLIE ATE HER fill. Jonah had shut down his computer and refocused his attention on her. They lay in bed, leftover dishes scattered on the dresser, bedspread crumpled at the foot of the bed. Jonah's arm was her pillow. She kept hearing Win's words, but before she could even think about taking things further with Jonah, she decided she really needed answers.

"What's wrong?" he asked.

"Nothing."

"No, it's something. What is it? You get this look like something's bothering you. Talk to me. You were always able to talk to me."

She closed her eyes. *Here goes nothing. Or everything.* "Earlier, you said that I make things easy. If that's true, why did you leave?"

"I graduated."

That was a cheap answer. "You left without a good-bye."

His muscles bunched beneath her, and she braced herself for a lie.

"I was worried about you. You were on self-destruct mode, and I didn't know how to stop you. You're this fucking brilliant person, Charlie, and you were going to throw that away. I saw all this potential totally going to waste. And for what? Some revenge that went nowhere? You couldn't bring Sylvie back."

She turned her face and laid it on his chest to avoid opening her eyes and seeing him. "But I could stop him from treating some other girl that way."

"Sure, you could stop him from posting pictures of other girls. But for how long? That's just it. I was afraid you'd give up your whole life to keep tabs on that guy. You couldn't change who he was. He didn't deserve that much of your energy." He traced a finger over her face—her eyebrows, the bridge of her nose, her jaw.

He'd left for the exact reasons she believed: She was a loser. She hadn't been good enough for him. She should feel better for having the conversation, for being told the truth. "I guess I owe you a thank-you."

"For what?"

She pushed off his chest and stared into his eyes. "You leaving made me realize how pitiful my life was. I had no balance. Nothing I really cared about. Losing you showed me I needed to unfuck myself. So I did."

"No, Charlie, you changed because you were ready to. And I'm really glad you did."

The deeper they got into this conversation, the more difficult it became to stay put. She didn't know why she was there, and his words only deepened the confusion. If he saw this as a fun weekend of catching up and great sex, she might not like it, but she could accept it. But now he talked about being glad she'd changed.

How little he knew. If he found out about her dropping out of school, his theory of wasted potential proven, she didn't want to see the disappointment on his face.

"I'm going back to my room," she said, scooting off the bed.

He sat up quickly. "What? Why? It's the middle of the night."

"I have to come up with a plan for tomorrow's competition."

"I can help you strategize. Who do you think you want to partner with?"

She stepped into her pants. "I can't accept your help. That would be cheating. I know you. Before sending invitations to any of these hackers, you would've vetted them. You know more about them than I do, and that would give me an unfair advantage." She pulled her shirt on and stuffed everything else into her bag.

"What about tomorrow during the day?"

"What about it?"

"Do you have plans?"

"Yeah, I need to do some networking, check into job possibilities."

"I'll see you on the floor then."

The offer seemed odd. Jonah hated the crowds. He preferred to face his screen attacking a problem. Unless he was recruiting as well. He'd said companies might want to hire competitors from the hackfest. He might know who was looking to hire. "Want to meet for a late breakfast? Then maybe you can introduce me to people you know."

"I can work with that." He stood as she slung her bag over her shoulder. "You sure you don't want to stay?"

"I need to go." *Before I get in any deeper.*

He walked her to the door, but before he opened it, he asked, "I forgot to ask. How did you know it was Maverick?"

It took a moment for her brain to register that he was asking about the competition. "A couple of things. First, when Poison started yelling, I did something you're not good at: I read faces. Most people in the room looked worried and agitated. Some were afraid of being falsely accused, more worried about whether someone screwed with their work as well. A couple of people were confident because they knew they were innocent. But Maverick was smug."

"I scanned the room, but Maverick wasn't facing me. I missed it. What else?"

"I watched him work. He was twitchy." She put up her hand to stop whatever comment Jonah planned to make. "I know everyone has their own process, but in the first challenge, he sat next to me. He was the second done, after Poison. I watched him work then too, and his movements were smooth, fluid. He was like a squirrel tonight. My gut told me he was guilty."

Jonah nodded. "I bet if we let you look, you would've found the same trail I did."

She shrugged. "I guess we'll never know because you didn't give us that chance. It might've been a good follow-up challenge, don't you think?"

Jonah watched Charlie walk down the hall to the elevator. He had no idea what had changed from the time she arrived to a few minutes ago, but it had. She'd planned to spend the night with him. He replayed the conversation in his head. She'd asked why he left and he was honest. Back then, she'd been lost, and no matter what he did, he couldn't stop her.

As it turned out, he did. He didn't believe that he was the sole reason for her getting her act together, but he couldn't help but wonder what would've happen if he hadn't left. Where would they be now?

He locked his door and flopped back on the bed. He almost blurted out that he couldn't have watched her wander that path three years ago because he'd loved her. After seeing her again, he began to think he still might. Being with Charlie was like coming home.

He didn't know why she wanted to escape his room and his bed tonight, but they had plans for the morning. He'd take her around and introduce her to the few people he knew, but there was no way he'd let them hire Charlie out from under him. He'd have to wait until after the hackfest to offer her a job, otherwise it might look hinky, but he would be offering one.

Mentally, he began composing an e-mail to Kyle about hiring prospects. He truly believed Charlie would be a good fit for the company, but he had to be upfront about their relationship.

In a relationship with Charlie again. Who would've thought?

~

THE FOLLOWING MORNING, CHARLIE WASN'T dressed in costume, for which he was grateful because kissing her with paint on her face had been gross. But she also wasn't dressed like a hacker in disguise. She wore a blazer over her dark jeans, and instead of her usual sneakers, she wore a pair of heels. Low heels, so she could maneuver, but still sexy.

"Hi." He greeted her with a kiss, and he was happy that she returned the affection.

"I figured we could just grab a coffee and a doughnut at the counter. I have a list of people I want to see today." She led the way to the coffee kiosk outside the hotel's restaurant. While she walked, she handed him a paper. "Do you know any of these people?"

He scanned the list. He'd come across some at other conferences, but he wouldn't say he was friendly with any of them. He knew them well enough to recommend her for a job and they would listen, though. "Some."

They ordered coffee, and instead of sitting at one of the tables as Jonah hoped, they walked back to the con floor. Charlie inhaled her doughnut and charged ahead. He had no idea why she invited him to tag along because that was all he was basically doing, following her. She didn't need his help for anything.

Charlie fearlessly introduced herself to people, chatted up a storm, and then passed her business card on. She was better at networking than most people he knew. One more reason why Kyle should hire her. And judging by the interactions she was engaged in, Kyle had better move fast. Charlie wouldn't be jobless for long.

As she finished up a conversation, he stood

beside her and grabbed her hand. "So do you have any preferences for where you want to work?"

"What do you mean? I just want a real job."

"I mean, are you willing to move out of Chicago?"

Her eyebrows furrowed. "I guess. I didn't give it too much thought. I just want to get my foot in somewhere, anywhere. If that means I work remotely from my apartment in Chicago, cool. If it means that I have to move somewhere else, or travel for work, I'll do it. I'm just tired of not doing anything real, you know?"

He remembered the restless feeling months before graduation, being ready to move forward with life. Although, for him, those months were tempered with Charlie, who confused him more than anything. He'd wanted to move forward, but he'd wanted her more. "Yeah. I get it. You never told me what field you want to get into. I'm assuming you'd want software, but are you looking to develop, write story, graphics, security..."

He hoped security. Not only would she do well at it, but he knew Kyle was looking to fill that position.

"Definitely not graphics. I can't draw for shit. That hasn't changed. I like writing, creating stories, but I don't think that's necessarily where I want to be. Not that I would turn down a job, but I don't have the portfolio for that. I think security is the way to go. I like being a problem solver."

Yes. He threw his arm around her shoulders and pulled her in for another kiss.

"What was that for?"

"I like kissing you." He wanted to pull her away from networking and take her back to his room, but even he could recognize that as a dick move. He also couldn't offer her a job without Kyle's approval. "I have to head back to my room for some work. Want to meet me later before the last competition?"

"That's real subtle, Best. You could at least offer to buy me dinner."

He smiled, thinking of the various ways they could spend time before the competition. "We'll order room service."

"Maybe."

He tugged her close again and gave her another kiss that melted the smirk from her mouth.

When he pulled away, she grinned. "Okay, you win. I'll see you later." She smacked his ass and walked away.

Jonah watched her leave and catalogued the reasons Kyle should hire her. Saying that she was smokin' hot probably shouldn't top the list, but his dick wouldn't let him forget it.

CHAPTER NINE

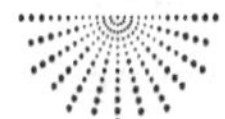

Charlie lay dozing in Jonah's arms again. The sun had set, and she needed to get ready for the competition, which meant leaving the warmth of his body and going back to her room to change. Although Jonah loved the heels she'd been wearing—enough that they stayed on her feet the first time they fucked before dinner— she didn't need her fellow hackers to be thinking about her shoes.

Jonah's fingers trailed lazily down her back, the soothing motion lulling her to doze again. This man was so good and so very bad for her. With other guys, she never had a problem jumping out of bed and out the door. Jonah made it difficult.

He shifted so she felt his erection against her back as his hand moved across her stomach. He said nothing as he raised her leg and brought it backward to rest over his, opening her to his touch. He played with her body, not talking, or asking, but demanding she give him everything.

One strong arm was banded under her and curled around her breasts, plucking at her nipples; his other hand began stroking her already wet pussy. His movements were slow and languid. He eased himself lower and entered her from behind, still moving like a thief waiting to be caught.

She closed her eyes and let him take her away to a place where soft and slow could shatter her as easily as hard and fast. Her body loved his every touch, and she wanted to tell him, needed to tell him, but the words strangled in her throat.

"I love your body," he whispered into her neck. "The way it answers every touch I give." His warm breath skated across her skin. "It's almost as sexy as your brain."

She couldn't respond because the sensations were too much, but she joined her hand to his, where they gave each other pleasure, quiet, calm, and safe.

Charlie hadn't been so scared in all her life as she was when she stirred after Jonah's lovemaking. She slid away from him. "I have to get changed for the competition," she whispered.

He stretched out in the bed, and she tried not to drool over the sight. She dressed quickly to stop the temptation of jumping on top of him, but then crawled back across the bed. "That was… amazing. More than I expected."

She kissed his chest and felt his heart thump beneath her lips.

"Will you come back here after the competition tonight?"

"You know as well as I do, we might be

working all night." She swallowed hard with the realization that this might actually have to be good-bye. "What time are you leaving tomorrow?"

"My flight leaves in the evening, but I have my room for the day. Business expense, so I don't have to check out."

Not much of an invitation, and Charlie wasn't sure if she could come back and spend the night with him, knowing he was leaving.

She stood and he walked her out, always the gentleman. Leaving his naked hips tucked behind the door, he grabbed her collar and hauled her in for another searing kiss. "I hope you know that I won't be able to think for shit tonight because I'll only be imagining you naked in my bed."

She patted his cheek. "Definitely good that you're not competing then, right?"

Back in her room, Charlie showered and changed. She pulled her hair into pigtails as she did for her Laura Nim costume and hoped it might bring her luck. Walking down to the conference room, she tried to decide if she wanted to partner with Jane. She'd brushed the girl off last night because she'd been too preoccupied thinking about Jonah. The truth was, Jane hadn't made much of an impression on her.

At the conference room door, Charlie took a deep breath. This was it. Last challenge. Jane was already settled in front of her laptop.

"Hi, Jane. Did you still want to partner up?"

Jane blinked up at her. "Oh, hi. Sorry. I didn't get the impression that you wanted to work with me, so I'm partnered with Dark Horse over there." She hitched her chin at a tall guy across the room.

Well then. "Okay, thanks anyway." Charlie backed off and went to check out the rest of the competitors. No way would she want to work with Poison. While he might be one of the best, she'd never be able to stomach his attitude and arrogance. Competitors' names were listed on the screen in front of the room. Cracker and Dark Horse were already side by side as partners. Poison and Virus were paired. That left Charlie with Crash, Override, Wyred, CyberRe4per, or Legend. As she stared at the names, CyberRe4per and Legend connected.

Charlie needed to make a decision fast, or she would have no choice at all. The problem was, she had no idea who was who. She couldn't match a face with a name, but there was only one other guy in the room hanging by himself. She shrugged and went to introduce herself. "Hi, I'm Rook. Are you partnered up yet?"

He extended a hand. "Override. And no, I'm not."

Override...if Charlie remembered correctly, he came in ahead of her and right behind Poison once Maverick had been booted out. He wouldn't be a bad choice. "Want to hook up?"

As the question left her lips, Jonah walked in. His gaze pinned her and she couldn't help but smirk. She knew how the question sounded, but she didn't care.

"Why not?" Override answered. He grabbed his laptop and followed Charlie to a section of table big enough for them to sit beside each other.

Jonah walked the perimeter of the room, watching as hackers set up and paired off. Charlie met him at the front of the room, where Carl was manning his laptop. "Hi." She winked at Jonah but spoke to Carl. "Rook and Override are partnering."

"Will do." Carl tapped the keys to put them together on the list.

Charlie took her seat again and waited. Waiting was the hardest part, which was why she never showed up early. She shifted in her chair and faced Override. "So, did you hang out at the con much?"

"A little. What's your game?"

"*The Order of Resskaar*. How about you?"

"I'm more into the comics, but I'll play some games. Never heard of *Resskaar* though." He stretched out his long legs under the table and opened his arms, resting one on the back of her chair.

Jonah's gaze burned into the back of her head. What the hell was his problem? He was leaving tomorrow, but he was going to get pissy because she talked to her teammate? She ignored him and continued to talk comic books with Override as the remaining competitors came in. They looked like they had already paired off, so Charlie had made a good choice in approaching Override.

Carl stood and started instructions for the night. "As you know, we're doing capture the flag for our last challenge."

Charlie loved CTF. She'd been honing her attack skills for months. She hoped Override could take over defense if she focused on attacking the others.

Her thrill was short-lived as Carl continued.

"Since the winner will get an all-expense paid trip to Def Con, and they do CTF attack/defense there, we decided to do Jeopardy style here."

A few groans echoed in the room.

Carl waved his arm for everyone to settle down. "Each team will be given the same set of tasks. You'll accumulate points for each task. They do *not* have to be done in order. We go until we have a winner. Any questions?" He looked around the room as everyone stretched and cracked knuckles, popped the top on energy drinks, and stole furtive glances across the table. "Okay, and...start."

Charlie looked over the tasks at hand. "I'm thinking the lower point tasks are going to be easier, so maybe we should divide the list and each conquer half. Sound good?"

Override nodded and they both started.

A running tally of points rolled next to each team on the screen at the front of the room. Forty minutes in, Charlie and Override remained in second place behind Poison and Virus. At the two-hour mark, they were still trailing Poison, but only by ten points. Charlie's blood raced. This was a possibility.

Suddenly, Jane shot up and yelled. "Cheat!"

Everyone froze, just as they had yesterday when Poison jumped up. This was getting ridiculous. Working in here was like being with first-graders.

Carl stood. "What are you talking about?"

"Rook is cheating. There is no way she can be that far ahead of everyone."

It took a second for Charlie to realize that she was being called a cheater. She stood. "What?" She looked up at the board. She and Override were still in second place, now only by five points, but Jane and her partner were fifty points behind.

"She had an unfair advantage. I wasn't sure, but I suspected. It's just not possible."

Charlie glared at her. "I am not cheating. How could I?"

A nasty smirk stole across Jane's face. "Someone fed you the answers."

Charlie's heart sank. She knew exactly where this was going. "No one gave me anything."

"Should we ask your boyfriend over there?" She pointed at Jonah sitting by the door.

"First of all, he's not my boyfriend. Second, he didn't give me shit. I've worked through each task just like everyone else."

Jane crossed her arms and waited. Carl looked back and forth between Jonah and Jane.

Jonah slid from the stool. "I didn't give her anything. I didn't create the challenge. Carl did."

Of course, Jonah wouldn't lie about their relationship.

Carl crossed the room to talk to Jonah. The harsh whispers carried across the room. Carl was asking about having a personal relationship with a competitor. Jonah nodded. She was screwed.

Her stomach sank. There was no coming back from this. "Fuck this." She slammed her laptop shut and looked at Override. "Sorry if you get screwed here too. I did not cheat, but I refuse to get thrown out for doing nothing wrong."

She slid her computer into her bag and rushed out the door.

"Wait," Jonah called.

She didn't, but then he caught her by the arm. "What are you doing?"

Charlie yanked her arm from his grasp. "I'm not going to sit there and be accused of cheating because I slept with you."

"Carl wasn't going to throw you out. He knows I didn't have access to anything he created."

"Doesn't matter. If I win, everyone in that room will question whether it was legitimate. Thanks for fucking this up for me." She turned away, tears clawing at her throat.

"Whoa. What do you mean me? I didn't do a damn thing."

"That's right, you didn't. All you had to do was deny we had any kind of relationship."

"Why the hell would I do that? I know you didn't cheat, and lying wasn't going to change that accusation."

"Whatever." She took a couple more steps before he moved in front of her.

"What's the big deal? It's a stupid small-time hackfest."

"Not for me it wasn't. I needed this win."

"Charlie, you have to know that you didn't really have a chance against Poison."

Tears welled and burned her eyelids. "Thanks for the vote of confidence. I guess we'll never know now."

She tried to push past him, but he laid a hand on her shoulder. "Why are you so upset?"

Charlie swallowed hard. "I needed this win. This was my chance. The prize is Def Con. I can't afford to get to Vegas and pay for a hotel and shit. And I need Def Con to network and find a job."

"No, you don't, Charlie. You're good enough that all you have to do is send out your résumé after graduation. You won't need to network. The jobs will be there."

She swiped at her face, hating every tear that fell. "No, they won't because there won't be a graduation. I dropped out."

He looked stunned, his mouth hanging open, and Charlie skirted around him. She couldn't look at his face knowing in a moment it would be filled with disappointment. She raced to her room, packed her stuff, and checked out to go back to her regular life.

JONAH STOOD STARING AT THE SPOT WHERE Charlie had stood. He couldn't have heard her right. Why would she have dropped out of school?

From down the hall, he saw Carl stick his head out the door of the conference room, looking for him. Jonah looked over his shoulder where Charlie had taken off and then back to

Carl. He had a job to do, and as much as he wanted to go after Charlie, he needed to see this through.

"Is she gone?" Carl asked.

Jonah nodded.

"Well, what do you think we should do?"

"Let Override keep the points accrued and work alone."

Carl patted Jonah's shoulder. "I explained that as a separate entity, I created the challenges and you had no access. She could've stayed."

Jonah shook his head. "No, she had a point. No matter what we said, the other players would always have their doubts."

They went back in to restart the game. Jonah was kicking himself for the entire episode. While he wouldn't have given up a moment of the time he'd spent with Charlie this week, he could've been more discreet, which is what she'd suggested in the first place. He hadn't thought it a big deal because he couldn't have helped her win even if he'd wanted to. He should've thought more about how hard it was for her, as a woman, to just be there.

He'd make it up to her after she calmed down. He'd already e-mailed Kyle about hiring her, and although she wouldn't be getting a degree, it shouldn't stop Charlie from getting a job. Plenty of places hired people without degrees. She had the skills.

Which was what she was proving by participating in the hackfest. She hadn't been an active part of the hacking culture in a while, not that he'd seen anyway, but she was reentering, hoping to use it as a gateway for a career.

Why the hell hadn't she told him?

That question nagged him for the remaining hours of the hackfest. Of course, Poison had won, but Override had been able to hold on to second place, much to the dismay of Cracker, the girl who accused Charlie. As soon as players started packing up their computers, Jonah edged out of the room.

He needed to see Charlie, to talk to her and tell her about the job he hoped to offer her. At her room, he knocked, but she didn't answer. He knocked harder. "Come on, Charlie, I know you're pissed, but let me in."

She still didn't answer, so he went back to his room. He picked up the phone and called her room, hoping she'd answer, but she didn't. He tried the bar where he'd met her the first night of the con and even asked her friend Derek if he'd seen her.

Derek delivered the news that she'd stopped briefly in the bar over an hour ago to say good-bye. She'd checked out of the hotel.

Jonah didn't even have her cell number to call her. He'd thought he had time for that later. They had one more night together. At least that was the plan. He'd thought they would celebrate and maybe make plans to continue seeing each other. With the school year almost over, he figured he could fly in to see her a couple of times or she could come to him. Of course, the school year didn't matter now since she wasn't enrolled.

As he walked back to his room, his phone jangled letting him know that someone was engaging Win. Charlie. He never came clean about his online persona either. He logged in to the game and tried to plan what to say. If he revealed himself now, she'd hate him. It was something that needed to be done face-to-face.

Win, you around?

Hey, gorgeous. How are things?

I'm such an unbelievable idiot.

I have a hard time believing that. What happened?

Remember my ex? Well, I went beyond stupid with him. I fell for him all over again thinking I could trust him since we've both done some growing up. But at the first bit of bad news about me, I realized I was wrong.

What do you mean? What could you have possibly said? Jonah's brain scrambled trying to figure out what he'd done to make her think she couldn't trust him.

Let's just say I disappointed him. Again. I have a habit of not living up to my potential. Laura grabbed Win's arm. *Let's go start a fight and steal some loot. I think I'm ready to finish the missions here and move on to a new game.*

What? It was bad enough that she left him in real life, but now he was supposed to let go of her in the game too? No, he'd find a way to extend their relationship here until he figured out how to fix things.

CHARLIE IGNORED THE E-MAILS SHE RECEIVED FROM Jonah. She should've reported him for hacking but since he worked for the software company that made *Resskaar*, he probably didn't have to hack. His words were kind enough. He apologized for not listening to her when she said that being seen together might cause problems for the competition.

Nowhere in the three e-mails did he mention their relationship or what he thought might happen. It was a pretty clear message that he no longer wanted to be with her since she was a failure. But the fourth e-mail, weeks after the con had ended finally prompted an answer from her.

Hey, Charlie, I'm pretty sure you're dodging my e-mails, and I don't know why, but I need you to contact me. Or better yet, contact my boss. He'd like to set up an interview with you later this summer. Unless of course, you've already found another job. In which case, let me know so I can tell Kyle that he screwed up by waiting too long.

She knew she needed to respond, but she didn't know what to say. The prospect of a real job was great, but she didn't want Jonah pulling some strings out of pity, like she couldn't do this on her own. Just like he thought she couldn't win the hackfest. She also wasn't sure that she could work in the same company as Jonah. It would be weird.

She sighed, fingers poised over the keyboard. But she could use this as leverage. No one had to know how she came about getting the interview. She typed back quickly that although she hadn't accepted any offers yet, she was keeping her options open. She asked for details about applying and what kinds of openings they had. The entire e-mail was very professional, even though her stomach flipped at the thought of sending it to Jonah. Within minutes of hitting send, she had a reply.

Ha! I knew that would get you to talk to me. Here's my number. Please give me a call. I don't like the way things ended between us (with you running away). Our conversation will have absolutely no impact on your interview or job. I really want to talk to you. I miss you.

Then he closed with links to the application forms she'd need to fill out.

Charlie stared at the words. She didn't know what to do. She wanted to call Felicity or Layla and ask them, but she still hadn't told them about dropping out of school. She made a resolution to come clean about everything as soon as they came home after graduation. They would start their new lives as adults with a clean slate.

In the meantime, she couldn't call Jonah. She didn't know what to say. Time away would be better. That way when they ran into each other at the company, maybe it wouldn't be so awkward. He'd move on and so would she.

From then on, every time she logged in to *Resskaar*, all she could think about was what she could add to the game to improve it. She knew the position she was applying for was security, but being that she knew the game after playing it from the beginning, she was certain that Jonah and his team would listen to her ideas.

Security would always be her first love, but part of her wanted to make the gaming experience better, especially for girl gamers. The stuff that Kraven pulled never should've happened, not that she blamed Jonah, but it was crap like that that made women shy away from gaming.

She began logging in many hours on forums talking to other women, understanding their experiences, and finding out what they wanted. She also continued to build her hacking skills, taking part in weekend events all over the city. Of course that meant that she often went into work on no sleep, but her customers didn't seem to notice.

The one person who had been cheering her on from the beginning was Win. They still met up for late-night battles and great conversations. He'd even convinced her to play the new beta version of the *Resskaar* sequel. She hadn't wanted to, simply because it made her think of Jonah, and she'd been trying to avoid that, but she could never say no to Win.

Kind of like she couldn't refuse Jonah.

The thought occurred quickly as she logged in for their nightly meeting. Jonah and Win were a lot alike. It certainly explained why she got along with Win so well. The game booted up, and she replayed conversations she'd had with Win over the months. They'd been in the same guild for over a year. He'd never done anything to make her think he was Jonah.

Surely, Jonah would've said something, right?

They'd talked about the game. Before she had time to type anything, though, Win was already talking.

Hey, gorgeous. Please tell me you're going to Def Con. I'll be there and I really want to meet.

Her heart sank. She wanted to go more than anything, but she knew she wouldn't have the money to afford it. But his offer set her mind at ease. Jonah wouldn't invite her as Win. *Sorry, I can't afford it.*

I have a room booked with two beds, and I'll cover your registration if you can get yourself here.

That's really nice of you to offer, but I can't take your money.

I just got a bonus and a raise at work. I have no one to celebrate with. Please. Plus, I feel bad that I didn't make it to Chicago.

Let me see how much it'll cost to get there. A bus would probably be cheap but would take forever. She thought of Felicity. Felicity had offered to pay for her to get to Texas for spring break. Maybe she'd ask Felicity for a loan. One plane ticket couldn't be that expensive. She hated borrowing from Felicity though. It was never a loan; Felicity wouldn't let her repay the money.

Charlie weighed her options. Def Con was in just a couple of weeks. She really wanted that experience. She'd be able to network with thousands of people. She huffed out a breath and called Felicity.

"Hey, Charlie. What's up?"

"Hi. I have a huge favor to ask."

"Shoot."

"Can you lend me money for a plane ticket to Vegas? I have a friend who is going to Def Con—you know, the hacker conference—and although I wasn't planning on going, he invited me to join him and share his room." Charlie toyed with her mouse and the lone pen on her desk.

"When is this conference thing?"

"The end of June."

"Excellent!"

Charlie held the phone away from her ear. Felicity wasn't usually much of a screamer, but when the girl let loose, she could shatter things. "Why is this excellent?"

"Because Layla's going to Vegas for a pool tournament. She wasn't going to tell anyone, but I pried it out of her. You both need to be in Vegas at the same time. I say we all go and get our vacation together since spring break was a flop."

"It might've flopped for me and Layla, but you had all our good luck." And it was about time Felicity had something good going. Everyone believed that since she came from a wealthy family, she led a charmed life. Charlie knew better.

"Shoot me an e-mail with the details of your conference so I can compare it to Layla's info. You guys can do your thing, and we can all meet up together after for an extended vacation. I can't wait."

Felicity disconnected, leaving Charlie feeling like she'd been struck by lightning. She knew Felicity had a great spring break and fell in love with a great guy, but she was uncharacteristically bubbly. Charlie didn't believe for a second that it was a girls' weekend in Vegas causing that kind of excitement.

Charlie sent the info to Felicity and e-mailed Layla to see what she thought about Felicity's weird excitement.

Then she went back to the game to let Win know she would see him in Vegas.

CHAPTER TEN

Jonah stood in the hotel lobby, trying to ignore the people rushing off to the casino to lose their money. Def Con was already in full swing and Charlie's plane had landed. He made sure Win let her know that he wouldn't be in until late tonight, but that a key would be available at the front desk. He'd stowed his stuff in Kyle's room until he talked to Charlie. Jonah planned to tell her everything, but he also knew he had some stuff to make up for.

He wasn't disappointed in Charlie. He wasn't sure where she'd gotten that idea, but he knew they wouldn't be able to get past it until he convinced her that he'd fallen for her every bit as much as she'd fallen for him. His plan would work despite the fact that it was a little manipulative. Standing like a freaking idiot in the lobby waiting to accidentally bump into Charlie hadn't really been part of his plan.

He checked his watch again just as she rushed by him. She hadn't even noticed him. Or if she did, she'd gotten better at faking it. He waited until she got her room key and was headed to the elevator.

"Hey—" He had to stop himself from calling her gorgeous like he had in Chicago. "Charlie. You made it."

She spun, her eyes wide with surprise. So she hadn't been faking not noticing him.

"What are you doing here?" she asked.

"Work. And play. After the hackfest in Chicago, I realized how much I missed the fun of hacking. I came with my boss. He's still scouting new talent." He paused for effect, as though the thought just occurred to him. "You know, since you're here, let me introduce you to him. We can get drinks later."

The elevator dinged, but she didn't move to get on. Her mouth opened like she planned to speak, but nothing came out.

"I wish you would've called me," he said quietly. "Can I walk you upstairs and maybe talk to you for a couple of minutes?"

"I'm meeting someone."

"Now?"

"No, I mean, I'm here with someone, sharing a room."

He smiled and shook his head. "As much as I love the idea of getting you naked, that won't be happening until we clear some things up."

She snorted at him. "What makes you think that would be happening at all?"

He shrugged. "I didn't say it would, just that it wouldn't until we talked. That's all I want to do.

Talk. I think you owe me that much, since you ran out of the hotel in Chicago without a word."

"Not a good feeling, is it?" Her stance relaxed and she tilted her head, assessing him. He knew he couldn't push talking to her alone. She was still too wary.

"How about this? There's a CTF attack and defense starting in thirty minutes. I could use a partner. Meet me and let's play a game."

Her eyes narrowed and he caught a hint of her anger. "Maybe you should find someone more like Poison. I wouldn't want you to have to carry me."

Shit. That's what set her off? "I don't want to work with Poison or anyone like him. You're an excellent hacker—"

"But not quite good enough, right?"

"Where are you getting this? I never said you weren't good enough, just that you couldn't beat him. No one had a shot at knocking him out. He had a ton more experience than you. From what I could tell, all the dude does is competitions."

She said nothing and just stared at him.

"I'm sorry if I made you feel like you weren't good enough. I spoke the truth, and maybe I should've thought about how it sounded, but I never had to censor myself around you before." He stepped closer, hoping his apology softened her a little. "How could you possibly believe that I don't think you're good enough? I taught you everything you know."

That caused a laugh, a real one. "Don't give yourself too much credit."

"Come on. Be my partner. Afterward, we'll go for a drink and talk and I'll find my boss. After that, if you don't want to see me for the rest of the weekend, I can make myself disappear in the crowds."

Her laugh faded to a crooked smile, like she wanted to fight it off. "You know, Best, I wish I could believe that. I'll meet you in twenty minutes after I drop off my stuff."

He grabbed her hand and wrote the room number for the CTF. She looked at it before stepping on the elevator. "You know I'll kick your ass if I show up and it's not really a competition."

"I would expect no less. See you soon."

The doors closed and Jonah breathed deeply. Step one, accomplished.

Of all the things he thought made her leave in Chicago, him thinking she wasn't good enough never crossed his mind. He thought she was pissed that their relationship might've bruised her reputation. He knew she was upset at the thought of him leaving town again without her. But how could she ever think she wasn't good enough? She'd proven herself repeatedly.

He went and bought a coffee for himself and Charlie and went to the CTF room and waited. He really hoped Charlie wouldn't blow him off. Five minutes of standing in yet another hallway for her and he got antsy. He should've followed her to the room and made sure she came back.

CHARLIE RODE THE ELEVATOR BACK DOWN AND stared at the number inked on her palm. What the hell was she doing? She was supposed to be here to meet Win and network, not waste more time with Jonah.

But when he suggested a round of CTF as his partner, part of her couldn't refuse, as always. He said he believed she was good, but she wanted, maybe even needed, to show him. She wasn't the same girl he first taught how to hack. She'd honed those skills and learned plenty of others.

Plus, Win had left a message that he wouldn't be arriving until tonight.

The elevator doors opened, and she wandered down the hall to find the right room. In front of the door, Jonah stood holding two cups of coffee. She took a minute and just stared at him. Her heart lurched and the pain of missing him returned. She'd grieved that loss for three years, but losing him in Chicago the second time had hurt much worse.

He suddenly lifted his head and his eyes locked on hers. His smile brightened his face as he walked over, and she really liked the sight of him coming toward her.

"Hey, I was beginning to think I'd have to hunt you down."

"I'm not even late. Don't trust me?"

"You seemed really pissed."

"Pissed isn't quite right."

"What is then?"

She took the coffee from him. "No talking now. Time to strategize."

In truth she couldn't deal with the emotional crap when she wanted to focus on winning. One challenge at a time. They entered the room together and checked in. Jonah let her choose their seats and she chose the darkest corner she could find.

"Still hiding?" he asked.

"I don't consider it hiding as much as disguise. They can't judge what they don't see."

"I personally like to see."

She felt his gaze roam over her entire body, and her skin warmed, but she said, "Kind of like a boring old rerun."

He leaned over, his breath brushing the shell of her ear. "Babe, there's not a damn thing boring about you."

In that moment, Charlie knew she was in the middle of a losing battle that she hadn't signed up for. The Def Con people called through the room and laid out the rules for the CTF competition.

Jonah leaned over again. "You want to attack and I'll defend?"

"I'm not sure. Kraven got past your defense on *Resskaar* a couple of months ago." His jaw dropped and she winked. "Just kidding, Best. Learn to take a joke."

The shot was meant to give her distance from him, but she hadn't wanted it to really bother him. She just needed him to stop flirting so she could think. She knew he wasn't at fault for what had happened with Kraven. Start was called and the competition began.

The amazing thing was that as soon as they

were in their zone, Charlie felt like she had three years ago when Jonah had taught her how to play and hack and have fun with it. They worked seamlessly, barely needing to speak. They knew each other's moves before the keystrokes were entered.

One by one, they knocked out each team. Two hours after starting, Charlie allowed the sounds of the room to filter back into her consciousness. She blinked and looked up from her computer screen. It took another minute for her to realize that they'd won. They beat every other team.

Jonah was already standing when she jumped out of her chair and into his arms. "Woo-hoo! We did it."

He caught her and held her off the ground as her arms wrapped around his neck. Other players came forward to offer congratulations, and she suddenly realized where she was. The display of affection in itself didn't bother her as much as the fact of who she was clinging to.

She loved having Jonah's hands on her, but she shoved the thought aside with a helping of aggravation and guilt. In the elevator, she'd promised herself that she would be Jonah's partner for this one competition and nothing else. She was here to meet Win. Win was a guy she could count on. He wouldn't leave her feeling inadequate.

Charlie knew this because he already knew almost all of her secrets.

She pushed away from Jonah to accept handshakes from other players, but he wouldn't let her get far. He held tight to her hand, interlacing their fingers. The room cleared out and Jonah pulled her along through the crowd.

Out in the hall, he still didn't release her hand. "That was fucking amazing. You're even better than I thought."

"You're not so bad yourself." She tugged her hand. "You can let go now."

"Nope. You promised me a drink and conversation. And I like holding you."

She sighed. "I'm not going anywhere. You want to talk, we'll talk. Not that I think there's much to say. But you don't need to hold my hand."

"I know I don't need to. I want to." He smirked at her. "Do I make you nervous?"

Hell yeah. "Of course not. I can handle you."

He led her to the nearest bar and wove through the crowd like a man on a mission. He pulled out a chair for her. When she sat, he asked, "Beer?"

"Sure."

Another man joined them and Jonah introduced him. "Charlie Castle, this is my boss, Kyle Zimmerman."

Oh shit. She wasn't ready for an interview right at this moment. She'd been sure that Jonah had used the conversation with his boss as a ploy to get her to the bar for a drink. She forced her hand out in front of her to shake. "Hi."

Kyle put his drink down on the table as he accepted her hand. "Nice to finally meet you. I've heard a lot about you."

She immediately turned to glare at Jonah, who had already disappeared to get drinks. She tried to loosen her tight smile. "I hope you only heard the good stuff."

He nodded and eased onto the chair across from her. "Jonah had plenty to say about you. So much, in fact, that I began to believe you were a figment of his imagination."

"He does have a good imagination, but I can assure you that I'm real." And really in need of a decent job.

"So I see. I was in the room while you and Jonah played Capture the Flag. You showed re-markable skill."

She blushed at the compliment. "Thank you. It was a lot of fun."

"You and Jonah made an excellent team."

She nodded. What could she say? They'd al-ways made an excellent team. She glanced over her shoulder again. Where the hell was Jonah with her beer?

"Here's the thing, Ms. Castle—"

"Charlie, please."

"Charlie, I have quite a few applicants who are more qualified than you and who have experi-ence through various internships. And they come with a completed college degree."

Charlie's stomach plummeted. She shouldn't have agreed to this meeting right now. She wasn't prepared for rejection. Not yet. She bit the inside of her cheek to keep the pain from showing on her face. "I understand."

"However, Jonah believes you have something his team needs."

Huh? *Focus, Charlie, something is happening here.* She gripped her hands together in her lap under the table. "Excuse me?"

"I've allowed Jonah to handpick his team because it works for him. As long as he continues to produce and I like the results, I don't care how he gets them. He's not an easy team leader, but I'm sure you already know that." He lifted his glass and sipped the amber liquid.

What she wouldn't give for a shot of something, anything at this moment.

"Are you offering me a job?"

"I am. Jonah can give you the specifics because you'll be working directly beneath him. Now that I've witnessed your work, I can understand what he sees in you. You'll need some training, but you have skills."

Holy fuck. She had a job offer.

"Think about it. Talk it over with Jonah. Let us know." Then he stood and walked away without giving her the chance to say anything, which was good because her mouth had forgotten how to work.

She stared at the empty chair across from her until Jonah filled the space, setting her beer in front of her.

He quirked an eyebrow. "Congratulations?"

She blinked and tried to think. She had a job, but it was only because of Jonah. She would have to work with him. No, *for* him. Could she do that?

She grabbed the beer and chugged half of it in

long gulps. When she set the bottle down, she could finally speak. "What the hell are you trying to do?"

"Get you to work for me."

"I don't need a pity job."

He set his beer down with a loud thunk. "Pity has nothing to do with this. I had already e-mailed Kyle about you back in Chicago before the entire cheating accusation fiasco. Shit. I wanted to hire you as soon as I watched you work through the first challenge. The second challenge sealed it. That's why I didn't want to help you network. I knew someone would snap you up and I want you on my team."

His words sank in, but her brain refused to process them. She scrubbed a hand over her face.

"I know we have some personal shit to get through. And believe me, we'll get to that. But no matter how that shakes out, Charlie, I want to hire you. You're the missing piece I need for my team."

She looked at him from in between her fingers still covering her face. Joy spread through her chest. He wasn't looking at her with pity, and he wouldn't lie about why he was offering her a job. But like he said, they had some personal shit to deal with. Her hands slid away and she stood. "I have to think about this. I appreciate the offer. I really do. But I'm not sure if the personal stuff is something I can get past."

She turned, but he grabbed her wrist. "Before you go, can you just tell me why you dropped out of school?"

The question wasn't one she'd expected, but having already told Layla and Felicity, she had her answer handy. "I couldn't hack it."

"Bullshit."

"No, not that I couldn't handle the work. It was more that I was bored. School was always hard for me because I easily get distracted, but in the beginning, I was learning. After Sylvie, when I met you, I learned how to focus my energy."

"Yeah, I remember that. Too much focus isn't all that good either."

"I figured that out. I took a semester off and learned." She winked at him. "You know, kind of like you wanted me to. I spent time with people who knew their shit. After that, school was a bigger struggle. I felt like they were trying to teach me to crawl, but I was ready to run."

She felt a little silly saying it out loud, especially to him, but he nodded.

He slid from his stool and stood beside her. He lowered his head to her ear. Blood zinged through her and every nerve tingled as he whispered, "Let me help you run."

CHAPTER ELEVEN

Jonah watched Charlie walk away from him again, and it about killed him not to go after her. She needed to think and he understood, but it also left him with nowhere to go because he still didn't have the balls to tell her he was Win. He planned to tell her after she'd accepted the job offer.

It never occurred to him that she might not say yes.

He stayed at his table, finished his beer, and ordered another. The gift he had specially made for Charlie weighed in his pocket. He'd imagined her jumping up and down with excitement over the job and then he'd tell her like it was a funny little story.

Suddenly he didn't think she'd see it that way. He'd underestimated her again. And if his stupidity cost him her both personally and professionally, he didn't know how he'd forgive himself.

Maybe Win should just blow her off. He could disappear as easily as he came into Charlie's life.

But he couldn't do that to her. As Jonah, he'd abandoned her three years ago. He reinvented himself as Win Abo to keep an eye on her virtually. She'd confided in Win, shared parts of herself, and he couldn't pretend that didn't carry a lot of weight. She deserved the truth.

Leaving a tip on the table, he headed upstairs to their room, practicing what to say. Everything sounded completely ridiculous and inadequate in his head, which meant it would be worse out loud. He held the key card in his hand and then shoved it back in his pocket.

Announcing himself as Win by letting himself in the room would probably get his ass kicked, so he knocked.

"Who's there?"

"It's me, Jonah."

She swung the door open and his mouth dried. She only wore a *Star Wars* T-shirt that he was pretty sure she had stolen from him. "What do you want, Best? I told you I needed to think."

"I know. I'm not here about the job. Not exactly. I think in order for you to make the best decision, all the cards need to be laid on the table, and that includes dealing with our relationship."

She cocked a hip out and crossed her arms, making the shirt ride dangerously high. "We have a relationship?"

"I hope so. Can I come in?"

She swung her arm wide and closed the door behind him.

"I have one question, Charlie, and then I have some stuff to say, but before we get into that, your answer to my question isn't going to change how I feel about you. I want you to know that going in. And I hope that not only do you feel the same, but that you won't hate me after I say what I need to."

She rolled her eyes. "You're talking in circles, Best. Get to the point."

He shoved his hands in his pocket and touched the necklace for reassurance. "Why did you leave Chicago without talking to me?"

Charlie plopped on the edge of the bed but looked him in the eye. "Mostly because I was mad. I blamed you because Jane accused me of being a cheater." Her hand flicked up. "I know it wasn't your fault and it could've been explained away, but I wanted someone to blame and you were handy."

Keeping his focus on her face was difficult because as she spoke the shirt kept wiggling higher and he desperately wanted to know if there was anything under it.

"But I was hurt. You told me I couldn't beat Poison, but I believed I had a shot. You cut me off without giving me a chance. You had no faith in me." She took a deep breath. "And then, the way you looked at me when I'd told you that I'd dropped out of school. All that disappointment. I just kept hearing you say that I was throwing away all my potential."

Her gaze dropped with the admission, and she stared at her hands in her lap.

"That wasn't disappointment. It was shock. I didn't know what to say. As far as not thinking you were good enough to beat Poison, well, I hadn't given that much thought either. I wasn't kidding when I told you that I'd already contacted Kyle about hiring you. I looked at that hackfest for what it was: a game. I'm sorry I let you down."

He lowered himself and took her hands. "I've never been disappointed in you. I've been afraid for you, worried about you, but never disappointed. Just the opposite. You amaze me."

"Pretty words aren't going to make me take the job."

God he wanted to kiss her, but he forced himself to step away and finish.

"What, no snarky comment about what else you have to offer?"

"I have plenty to offer and even more snark, but first, I have a confession to make." He pulled the necklace from his pocket and laid it in her lap. "I had this made for you."

She held the necklace in the palm of her hands and held it up. The intricate Celtic knot glinted in the lamplight behind her. "It...It's beautiful."

She hadn't yet made the connection, so he forged ahead. "I know you think that with the exception of some harmless online scoping, I haven't had any contact with you except in Chicago. That's not true. I've been playing *Resskaar* with you." He swallowed a lump and said, "I'm Win Abo."

Her hands dropped down to her lap. "What?"

"Win Abo. When I found you playing

Resskaar, I just wanted to check in on you, to know you were okay after I left."

She stood, one hand fisted tightly, the other still cradling the necklace. "So you pretended to be my friend? You've been lying to me for more than a year?"

He raised his hands in defense. "I never planned to be part of your life. I wanted to make sure you were okay, but then once I saw that not only were you okay, but you were Charlie, *my Charlie*, the girl I fell for three years ago, I didn't want to leave you again. I was afraid if I'd told you who I was, you'd leave *Resskaar* and I'd lose you." He stepped forward, knowing he was risking a punch to the face. "I knew I screwed up when I left after graduation and you probably wouldn't talk to me again, but if I could have the small part of you that played a game, I wanted it."

She backed away from him. "God, I'm such a fucking fool. Win Abo...Obi-Wan, right?"

He nodded.

"Oh God, I bet you had a hell of laugh in Chicago, didn't you?" She crumpled back to the bed. "I had such a brave front on when I saw you, but I went to Win and confessed to him how I felt seeing you again."

Tears brimmed on her lids and his heart broke. He didn't want to hurt her. Ever.

"I never laughed at you. I was afraid to tell you. I've never been more afraid of anything until this moment."

"Why?"

He didn't know what to say. He wasn't even

sure he knew what she was asking. He knelt in front of her again. "I love you, Charlie. I loved you three years ago, but you scared me. I couldn't watch you self-destruct. And you didn't. I should've had more faith in you back then. When I met Laura Nim in game, I knew she was you. The kick-ass attitude, the sense of humor, the loyalty and determination—it was all you, the best parts of you, the parts I fell for.

"It was never about making you feel foolish." Tears trickled down her face, and he reached up and brushed them away. "I planned to tell you in Chicago, after the last challenge. When you left, I couldn't tell you in an e-mail. You still trusted Win, so I used that. I won't apologize for that part. You were ignoring me. But I wanted this time to be different. No secrets, no games. Just us."

She took a shuddering breath. "What are you saying?"

"I still love you, Charlie. I want us to have a chance."

He took the necklace from her palm and held it up. "I designed this in the game just for you. It's one of a kind. The Celtic knot weaves endlessly, but in the center, there's the Claddagh. Love, loyalty, and friendship. You are the best of that for me."

Silence answered him. For the first time since he'd seen her again in Chicago, he began to doubt. His apology might not be able to overcome her stubbornness. She traced the lines of the knot and he held his breath.

"I don't know, Best. I'm not sure that a one of a

kind necklace is enough groveling to make up for spying on me and lying to me for almost two years." She reached up and clasped the necklace around her neck.

His voice was rusty when he spoke, but he tried not to jump with excitement. "What else did you have in mind?"

She stood, and holding his hand, pulled him up beside her. "I'm thinking a whole lot of worshipping of my body to start. And we'll have to work on your gaming skills, 'cause you know, Laura's been saving Win's ass for a long time."

Laughter burst from his chest and he scooped her up in his arms. "I'm open to any and all suggestions."

She laughed, and when he kissed her, it was like coming home.

Keep reading for a special excerpt from chapter one of *Her Winning Formula*, Felicity's story! And don't miss Layla's story in *Her Best Shot*, now available.

If you liked *Her Perfect Game*, be sure to check out Shannyn Schroeder's contemporary romance series, The O'Learys:

More Than This
A Good Time
Something to Prove
Catch Your Breath
Just a Taste
Hold Me Close

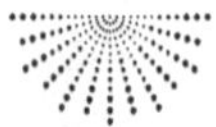

HER WINNING FORMULA

Felicity Stone eased her way past the crowd hovering by the boarding gate. God, how she hated airports. Most people were afraid of flying or crashing. For her, being crammed with over a hundred other people was torture. She sought out the farthest seat she could find while she waited for the announcement to board.

It had been bad enough that she had to switch planes, in Chicago of all places, but her first flight had been delayed. Her original thought when she found she had a connecting flight in Chicago was to convince her friend Charlie to meet her at O'Hare for lunch. Then, with any luck, she'd be able to convince Charlie she needed to go on spring break vacation even if it meant letting Felicity buy her plane ticket. The plane being late ruined that plan.

She huffed out her irritation and set her hefty backpack on the floor at her feet. She checked her phone and saw the text from Layla. Her car had broken down in Georgia. Felicity jumped from her seat. Another text said that her wallet had been stolen and included the license and picture of some guy that Layla had decided to go home with. What the heck was she thinking? Layla had always been too quick to trust. At least she left a trail of proof of who this guy was.

Felicity dialed Layla's number and paced. She'd barely gotten three feet when someone tapped her shoulder. She turned and looked up and up. The guy was probably about six feet tall, towering over her barely-over-five-foot height and had dark scruff covering his jaw. She widened her eyes in expectation of the reason for his interruption.

He lifted her bag from his side. "I think you left this—"

She blew out a breath and disconnected the call. "So what? I'm trying to make a call."

"The thing is, we're in an airport, and I really can't afford not to get to Texas on time."

"I don't control the plane."

"But a bag left unattended might get reported." He still had her bag, dangling from his fingers as though it weighed a few ounces.

"You're being a bit paranoid, don't you think? Every bag left sitting doesn't contain a—"

His other hand quickly covered her mouth. "I will pay you twenty dollars to not finish that sentence. Department of Homeland Security and the TSA do not take kindly to that word being used in an airport."

She swiped his hand away from her and

snatched her bag away from him. Swinging it over her shoulder, the weight pulled at her back.

The guy looked at her and smiled—seriously smiled—and then put out his hand. "I'm Lucas, by the way, and I'm normally not so paranoid, but I have a wedding to get to, and if this plane doesn't leave on time, my family might kill me."

"So are you going around policing all of the passengers, or just me?"

He dropped his hand and shrugged. "I noticed your bag and was afraid it might be a problem. Sorry I bothered you."

He turned and walked away, taking the seat two over from where she had staked out her spot. There were four other seats in that row. Did he have to sit within touching distance of her? Felicity took a deep breath. She knew her thoughts were slightly unreasonable. The stress was getting to her.

Layla was stuck in Georgia, but she'd be okay until Felicity landed and could get her some cash. Another deep breath. Layla would *not* leave her to attempt to do spring break on her own. She and Layla went to school mere miles from each other but hardly ever hung out. Their schedules were hectic, so Felicity was really looking forward to spring break. This would be their last spring break since they were all graduating, except Charlie who needed an extra year. By this time next year, Layla would be working at the NSA doing mysterious government security and Felicity would be working at her father's lab in the R

& D department developing her own perfume. Frivolous vacations probably wouldn't happen.

Felicity walked back to her seat and wrestled her textbook from her bag. Working out equations would soothe her and ease the gnawing stress. She was scribbling furiously through an equation when she felt another tap on her shoulder. She glanced up and saw the guy staring at her again.

"They're boarding. You were pretty engrossed in what you were doing."

She blinked rapidly to clear the numbers from her mind. He turned and walked away. She slammed her book closed, and in looking at her watch, realized that she had been working for more than twenty minutes. She watched the guy step into the boarding line. He probably thought she was crazy, or maybe stupid. She shoved her book back in her bag and got in line.

As if sensing her presence, the guy—what the hell was his name?—turned again and looked down at her. "Business or pleasure?"

Now that she really paid attention to him without irritation poking her, she realized he was cute. His dark hair was a little messy, but his blue-gray eyes somehow managed to be both inviting and piercing. "Huh?"

"Are you going to Texas for business or pleasure?" He'd slowed his rate of speech like he was speaking to someone without command of the English language.

"Pleasure. Spring break with a friend."

His gaze wandered down her body and back up to her face. "What school do you go to?"

"Harvard."

His mouth opened, he paused, and then did it a couple of more times. Now who looked like he didn't know English?

"South Padre Island?" he finally asked.

She nodded. The line shifted forward.

"You'll love it. It's a lot of fun."

The flight attendant at the gate asked for his boarding pass and welcomed him aboard. Felicity handed over hers as well, grateful to finally be getting on the plane. Not that she should be in a hurry now since Layla wouldn't be arriving for at least a few days. A sharp spear of panic hit her. What was she supposed to do alone for days?

Once on the plane, Felicity hooked left, suddenly aware that she was following the tall guy. She paused to make sure she was, in fact, in first class. The flight attendant looked at her pass and pointed toward her seat to confirm she was going the right way. As she walked down the aisle to her seat, Felicity saw the same darn guy in her spot. She absolutely couldn't catch a break today.

"Excuse me, you're in my seat."

He stood, checked his pass, and looked at the window seat beside him. He smiled at her again, this time flashing teeth and a dimple in his right cheek. Damn, he was cute. "Is there any way you would consider switching with me? Even in first class, my legs are cramped. Being in the aisle allows me a little more space."

The smile dazzled her enough that it took a

minute to process what he was saying. She didn't want to give up her aisle seat. Taking the window seat effectively trapped her.

A little voice in her head said that there were worse things to be trapped by than a hot dude with a killer smile.

"Fine. Whatever." She stepped aside so he could move and she slid into place by the window.

"Would you like me to put your bag up for you?"

"No. I'll keep it here." She smashed it under the seat as best she could. She would definitely need to be able to work some equations to get through this flight sitting next to him.

He took his seat. "Sorry, I didn't catch your name earlier."

She leveled a look at him. "I didn't give it."

His mouth slid into a half smile, enough to let the dimple peek. "I think we got off on the wrong foot. Hi, I'm Lucas. May I ask your name?"

"Felicity."

"Nice to meet you, Felicity."

She buckled her seat belt and willed the pilot to get moving.

"So, Harvard, huh? Where are you originally from?"

"Chicago."

"I'm from Chicago too. Small world. What's your major?"

"Chemistry." Even as she answered him, she knew he was trying to carry on a conversation and she should do more, but she wasn't good at it.

The flight attendant did her usual safety speech, and the pilot announced they were ready for takeoff. Lucas buckled himself in and suddenly got quiet. The plane began to move, and Felicity felt the waves of tension coming from her seatmate. She looked at him from the corner of her eye. He had a death grip on the armrest, his knuckles white.

"Are you okay?"

He nodded.

She turned back to look out the window.

"Actually, no, I'm not. I don't like to fly."

"It's no big deal. The flight will only be a few hours."

"The takeoff and landing are what get to me. My kids have a habit of rattling off statistics, and one of them told me that almost thirty percent of crashes occur during that time."

"Kids?"

"I'm a teacher."

She studied him. She'd never had a teacher who looked like him. "Gym?"

"Special ed."

That surprised her. She couldn't imagine him in a room full of rowdy, out of control kids or kids who had a hard time learning. Gym teacher she could picture. He looked like the athletic type.

"I'm also the baseball coach. Which is why I didn't want to come on this trip. I had to leave my assistant coach in charge of practice while I'm gone."

She couldn't believe he was nervous. He continues to carry the conversation effortlessly. "Whose wedding?"

"My brother's. He met his fiancée in South Padre and they decided to have a destination wedding. And of course, it had to be over spring break."

"I guess you didn't have a choice to skip it since it's your brother."

He laughed. The warm, rich sound tickled through her and she couldn't help but smile back.

A small ping let them know they could release their seat belts, so Felicity did. "Takeoff is done," she whispered.

Meeting His Match

Daring Divorcees Series

One Night with a Millionaire

My Best Friend's Ex

My Forever Plus-One